Praise for the Inspector Kenworthy Mysteries by John Buxton Hilton

Books by John Buxton Hilton

HANGMAN'S TIDE
FATAL CURTAIN
PLAYGROUND OF DEATH

CRADLE OF CRIME
(coming in May)

PLAYGROUND OF DEATH

JOHN BUXTON HILTON

DIAMOND BOOKS, NEW YORK

A hardcover edition of this book was published in 1981
in Great Britain by William Collins Sons & Co. Ltd.

PLAYGROUND OF DEATH

A Diamond Book / published by arrangement with
the author's estate

PRINTING HISTORY
William Collins Sons & Co. edition published 1981
Diamond edition / February 1991

ISBN: 1-55773-461-5

Diamond Books are published by The Berkley Publishing Group,
200 Madison Avenue, New York, New York 10016.
The name "DIAMOND" and its logo
are trademarks belonging to Charter Communications, Inc.

PRINTED IN THE UNITED STATES OF AMERICA

10 9 8 7 6 5 4 3 2 1

PLAYGROUND
OF DEATH

• 1 •

SUPERINTENDENT BARTRAM WAS an eager man, moon-faced about the jowls, incipiently pop-eyed: incipiently hyper-thyroid. He was well aware of himself as a wit: though perhaps that was doing him less than justice. His deadpan comments could be a personal strength: there were delayed-action barbs on some of his shafts. Nor did Kenworthy fail to notice that five out of his first six stories had been against himself; he believed in disarming the opposition in advance.

The Filton-in-Leckerfield police station was a new one. He came round from behind his recently issued beechwood desk, on to his recently issued pocket handkerchief of black-and-white check carpet. Evidently the next anecdote was going to need some kind of demonstration.

"Couple of months ago: HM Inspector of Constabulary paid an official visit. And you know what that does to a station. Or maybe you don't. Before he arrived I had a muster parade in the yard, and I could feel the tension twenty yards in front. So I stood them at ease, and before I walked round the ranks, I hitched my trousers up above my ankles."

He did it now, exposing the hairy gap above his socks.

" 'And I hope no one else on this parade has been such a berk as I have this morning,' I told them. I'd gone and put my bloody golfing socks on with my full dress uniform. Bloody great laugh went up, and we got through the day. They didn't have to snigger about me in corners. I'd *told* them."

More likely he'd put those socks on on purpose, rigged the whole incident. But it had worked. He might possibly be a very good copper.

"Do you know Lancashire at all?" he asked.

"Barely."

"You'll find no clogs and shawl in Filton. We reckon to be ahead of the times here: about six months, as a rule. When other spinning towns were taking a beating from man-made fibres and cheap imports from Hong Kong, the shrewd observer would have noticed that Filton-in-Leckerfield's mills had been taken over by light industry. They were mail-order warehouses, or even housing battery hens. Or else they had learned to spin nylon for themselves."

It was Kenworthy's impression, too, that he had come to a town that had its pride. The High Street had been given a Civic Trust face-lift in the sixties and pedestrianized in the seventies, when motorways to east and west had taken arterial traffic out of the town centre. The handsome stonework of the parish church had been scraped clean of a century's grime; and the present generation had probably noticed for the first time that it was handsome. There were red-brick mills, robust monuments of Victorian affluence. There were square-cut grids of terraced houses, not all of which had yet been cleared to make way for multi-storey car parks. But these things were beginning to look like mere show pieces of industrial archaeology.

"I shall also be handing you, Kenworthy, for your safe keeping, a set of golf clubs—"

It was clearly the point that he had been leading up to. Kenworthy jumped the mental gap.

"Bielby?"

Bartram nodded. "*Not* a gift, keen though he would have been for me to take them. An indefinite loan. If you lived and worked in a town like this on my salary and liked to play the odd nineteen holes with the chosen few, you might not be beyond borrowing."

Kenworthy said nothing.

"Apart from that, I've nothing on my conscience. At your service, Superintendent."

"Thank you."

Bielby had served Filton for two terms as mayor, once in the middle fifties, once in the sixties. Latterly he had done less in the Borough, more on the County Council, where the bulk of the money was spent.

"I've no doubt you're going to upset a bad bugger or two," Bartram said, "but by and large we like to think that we're a clean town. Safe and quiet for law-abiding folk to live in. That, according to my book, is the object of the exercise."

Bielby had also been Chairman of the Juvenile Bench, Vice-Chairman of Hospital Group Management, Past President of Rotary, *inter alia*. Then one night, a little less than a month ago, he had come home earlier than usual and shot his wife. That was the prosecution's simple and confident contention. There was plenty of good-neighbourly evidence that he was seldom as a rule home before midnight—and sometimes recently not at all; and that Margaret Bielby had herself taken to receiving late-night visitors. Then, that Tuesday, Bielby had come home slightly before eleven, not long after an unidentified car had been heard to leave his drive. There had been a shot; and Bielby had been discovered standing by the blood-soaked bed with a warm-barrelled pistol in his hand. It was a Walther 7.65 wartime German police model, and he did not deny that he had bought it in the black market and hung on to it after demobilization.

Bielby had been remanded for seven days in custody twice. The rumour was that in his remand cell he had fallen out with and dismissed his solicitor, that he was going to conduct his own case, and that he was delighted at the prospect of proclaiming his innocence as early and dramatically as possible.

"An extrovert," Kenworthy suggested.

"He'd bounce off a quarry bottom," Bartram said.

Because Bielby served on the Borough Bench, he was brought before the Rural District magistrates: a brittle distinction, since they shared the same new courtroom, which was packed for the hearing, as was the pedestrianized High Street. Bielby was brought in a highly polished midnight-blue Cortina, but all the bystanders saw was his blanketed shape. A groan went up from the pavements when it was seen that they were going to drive him into the yard and close the great gates before his official unveiling.

It would have proved easier to get Bielby out of the car before the blanket was removed. It caught between his thigh and the seat as he tried to swing a leg over the sill. Someone helped him to his feet.

And then a shot was fired.

It was shockingly sudden, echoing round the yard, thrown back from the stolid walls of the Tunnicliffe Brothers' warehouse, reverberating up and down the Civic Trusted High Street.

The impact knocked Bielby sideways against the rear quarter-light window. He jack-knifed down into a huddle, half the blanket under him. It was a struggle to get him free and he died within a minute or two: a ruptured aorta accounts for a lot of blood in a very short time.

It was not necessarily an indictment of Bartram's administration that a murder should take place in a yard that was under his direct command. Indeed, when the first report reached the Chief Constable's desk, it was still not known whether the trigger had been pulled on police premises or not. But all in all, the decision to have the affair investigated by outsiders, and a strong team at that, was not a hesitant one. That was where Kenworthy came in.

"There was a lot of other people's pie-crust under Bielby's fingernails?"

That was how Kenworthy opened the bowling.

"You wait till you read the crap that he's been putting down on paper to while away remand time," Bartram said. "He's been having a little go at auto-biography."

"I keep hearing about this. I'm dying to get my hands on it."

"You'll find the original, along with essential abstracts and first priority files, in the office that we've given you. If you need anything else, you know my extension."

• 2 •

BIELBY HAD WRITTEN on the close feint lines of a quarto size jumbo economy refill pad which he had had brought into Preston Prison for him. His handwriting was not in the contemporary fashion; there was a suggestion of conscious elegance about it.

In the days when the RAF was teaching me to fly, and I was sweating cobs through my first solo hours, it's curious how I used to get myself to sleep at night, picturing a swoop over Filton-in-Leckerfield, down through the grey filter that God kept between himself and the town. I'd hedge-hop over the copper turrets of the Prince Consort Mill, over the cowls of the Town Moor, down by the end-house hoardings, the Bovril and the Guinness and the Bisto, down over Swallow Street and Colliery Street and Elgin Row, down past the trees and the railings, till I could see the mud in the goal and the grey riddled slag under the swings and see-saws.

But my first view of St. Luke's Playground did not show me much of this. All I saw was a part of a part of it. I was four years old, and I could see it through a knot-hole in our yard gate when I stood on an upturned Brussels sprouts box. Till a voice—my mam's or my nan's—would come screeching round the old mangle, telling me to get down before I fell and broke a limb, which of course, I would only do to spite them.

They disagreed, those two, on every issue that arose in, round, under or between them, and by the time that I was four I was learning how to make the most of it. If it was liquorice I wanted, then it was my mam I had to upset; Pontefract cakes to my nan were what the holy wafer is to a Catholic. But if I wanted a handful of tigernuts from Armitage's stinking little shop, it was my nan's feet I had to get under. Old Armitage allowed my mam eighteenpence credit a week.

It was their hatred of each other that kept these two going. Even little things got on each other's nerves, like Adam's apples going up and down. My nan's teeth wouldn't stay in when she was eating a Chorley cake, and there wasn't a grip, clip or slide on the market that would keep my mam's hair up. But their antagonism went deeper than things like that. They hated the sight, sound and presence of each other. They went together to the cinema every Monday night, after the usual row about which one to go to. And when they got back, it had always been worse than one or the other of them had said it would be. If it was one's turn to cook the Sunday dinner, the other would see that we were out of salt or gravy browning. They'd rather have eaten a rotten meal than admitted liking a good one. It was the only bond between them, this mutual loathing. If you'd taken that away from them, they couldn't have lived together.

But then, it was hate that kept the Town Moor going. There's a lot of talk these days about the disappearance of the community spirit. The truth is that nowadays people don't get to know each other well enough to work up the right kind of ill-feeling. They live too far apart, so there isn't the same need to keep up pretences. We used to send Christmas cards next door and across the road, we boiled broth for one another when we were sick, we passed on what was left of the brown and purple filth in our medicine bottles, we handed on old baby-clothes, we brought one another into the world and we laid one another out.

But, by God, it was only one another's misfortunes that made life bearable. To see the old fever-cab, horse-drawn until well into the thirties, carting a diphtheria case from someone's door to the Isolation Hospital! To know that someone was pregnant after a bout of drink-fuddled sex that you'd heard through the party wall! And now and then there were great explosions of community triumph—as when old Mosley cut his throat in his coal-shed. When they had a whip-round for some poor bitch who'd been widowed by the fire-damp or the spinning-shed, it wasn't out of pity for her misfortune; it was to establish that it *was* a misfortune. It's only other people's misery that keeps your own barely tolerable.

That was the Town Moor. And I saw it through a knot-hole when I was four. Then one day the old sprout-box arse ended on me, as they had said it would, and I tore a great gash in my trousers. That

was when I found out my identity. One or the other of
them, my mam or my nan, opened the scullery
window and announced to anyone who was listening
that I was a bastard.

If you want to make a woman respectable—so respectable that she stands out like the Prince Consort
Mill's chimney—first put her in the family way, and
then move out of her orbit. And your chances of
success will be better if she happens to have a mother
with a face like a constipated ferret who bought her
false teeth over the counter of a pawn-shop. My nan
made my mam go on calling herself Miss Wheeler;
wouldn't let her wear a ring; wouldn't let her have
Martha Garbutt, who passed herself off round the
Playground as a midwife. She took charge of my
arrival herself, boiling water in the egg-pan, the
milk-pan and the porridge-pan, until she must have
had the top of the kitchen range red-hot to keep them
all going. And when I was straining to get through the
first of life's little knot-holes, she let my mam scream
her head off, so that Elgin Row did not have to ask
questions—they knew. And my mam went on screaming for two hours after I'd emerged, so that my nan
had to tell her to shut her daft gob, it was all over till
next time.

Either she'd got into the screaming habit, or else
she'd taken note of what she was henceforth stuck
with.

And how do I know all this? Because I heard it a
hundred thousand times. They never let rest for a
minute, those two; not for a week, a month or a
decade.

Respectability was the Playground's cage-cable and main hauling engine. It was all they had. It was respectability that made old Mosley cut his throat—it wasn't because he knew his time was up. He'd half a loaf of bread left, enough HP Sauce to ease a pie down. There was even a drop of milk left in his jug after he'd filled the saucer for his cat. And they found a sixpenny piece in the lining of his jacket. Some said he'd have put it off for another twenty-four hours, if it hadn't been for mislaying that tanner. But I don't think so. I think he wanted to show that he had enough gumption to get out of the game while he was still breaking even. You could tell that from the considerate way in which he had it all planned—he never was one for giving unnecessary trouble. He did it in his coal-shed, where there was a corner-heap of slack that soaked up all the blood and mucus. The Stringers and the Bennetts had that heap of slack between them. There was some thrifty housekeeping, round the Playground.

Respectability meant being told the stories of Noah's ark and Moses in the bulrushes when I was three and my mam was blackleading the grate. Respectability meant, oddly enough, not going to Sunday School with the other kids. That was because we were Chapel, not Church. We did not go to chapel either, but that was a complexity that nobody bothered me with. And it was always firmly drummed into me that being Church of England was not in itself a bar to respectability. It was only when you got to the Catholics that you traversed that pale. I'll say this for my mam: she was conscious of her moral responsibilities.

My nan was more respectable than my mam could ever be, because she had been married; in a chapel; to a Good Man, who wouldn't have demanded his rights until he'd signed for them in front of a couple of witnesses. There was a bloody great photograph of my grandfather in my nan's bedroom, in sepia, head and shoulders, with the sleeves of his tunic and the bandolier of Kitchener's Army fading away into a sort of artistic nothingness, roughly the size and shape of a lavatory seat. He had a sad, faraway look in his eyes, as befitted a man who had signed for my nan. But by and large, the first Earl of Ypres had not got much change out of John James Wheeler. John James had only been singing in the mud for five days, wearing a bullet-proof waistcoat that my nan had seen advertized in the *Daily Mail*, when he was persuaded to fix his bayonet and run across a field raked by machine-gun cross-fire. I used to think, when I looked at that portrait, that the remainder of his arms and most of his body below the nipples had been shot away in one great moment of heroic abandon. I also connected this with his permanent air of remote melancholy.

And it was towards the end of the war that my mam, to quote a phrase that my infant ears had been quick to scoop up, had had me by a soldier. This event has always fascinated me, and I have often pondered about the circumstances. I have seen a studio photograph of my mam at about the time when it must have happened, and the soldier concerned must have had a pretty sharp eye for original sin, if he spotted much promise in the pale skin drawn tightly across her forehead, the downward tilt in the corner of her mouth, and those sullen eyes.

However, he must have been an opportunist of sorts. And she must have been dead unlucky. I always assumed that she had only had sex once in her life, that in his own interests the soldier did it under cover of darkness, that it didn't last long, and that the only thing she got out of it was me. I don't like to think that it happened behind the goal-posts. There are some situations in which you don't like to picture your own mam.

If you wanted to see the Playground in its proper glory, you had to be there on Bonfire Night. If the Playground originally sprang from some conscious plan in the mind of mortal man, then its conception had surely been on and for a November evening. When a twopenny star-shell burst against the Reckitt's poster or the Cephos Salt placard, there was a new sheen on the slate roofs and a strange gleam on the slag at our feet. There may have been pinched and sallow faces amongst us, but we looked healthy enough in the glow of the embers as one or other stooped for a chestnut or a potato. More than half our pleasure was in anticipation and as early as the end of September you'd see the kids dragging half a tree across the shale, as soon as the Council started lopping branches in the Park. The moment we were let out of school, we'd be scouting round for inflammables; discarded roofing-felt from the sheds on the allotments—and some that hadn't been discarded—old mattresses, old tyres; we planned constructively, in terms of smoke and stink.

We shaped the whole thing up into a dark and cavernous wigwam, which had to be defended, even during school hours. So we used to put Sonny Simpson on a little stool inside the cave. Sonny was a perpetual adolescent from somewhere half-way down Colliery Street. I don't know whether he was an idiot, or a cretin, or a mongol, or an imbecile, or what. He had a footing in more than one classification. But we could rely on him to see that no one took as much as a twig off our fire. He used to sit there for hours in the half-darkness, his mouth open and slobber running down his chin, dipping an old kitchen ladle into a witch's cauldron of a coal bucket. Now and then he'd stir his brew up from the bottom: a mixture of sump-oil and mud and tar and piss, and any other liquid filth that we could find, and if any stranger came too close, Sonny would throw great dollops of it at him—all over his clothes, his face, his hair. Sonny did not care. He was daft enough for anything.

1930 wasn't a good year for economics—but it was the best year for fireworks that I remember. I'd done pretty well for myself, due to crafty management of the usual dissension in my camp. I'd even risked trundling an effigy in a truck round parts of the town where I wasn't known. So, being in funds, I had company: Billy Turner, Whacker Pearson, Micky Springett.

And, of course, what we were really playing at was War. When a Roman candle sent a ball of fire up over the railings, it was a Very light. The pungent fumes that wafted across from hostile family emplacements must have been reminiscent of the real thing. There

was in fact one poor old devil, down in Swallow
Street, said to be suffering from shell-shock, who
used to climb into his wardrobe twice a year and close
the door behind him—both times in November. Once
on the fifth, when we were at it, and once on the
eleventh, when the Territorials were making a pig's
dinner of the Last Post.

Bonfire Night, 1930; and I, Sid Wheeler, commanding remnants of my platoon, moved progres-
sively round the Playground, playing hell where hell
was effective, respecting those pockets of resistance
where there might be parkin or treacle toffee still to be
cadged. And we came at last on Maggie Leyland and
her mum, standing, as might be expected, a little
apart from the rest of the crowd.

To Billy Turner and Whacker Pearson, they seemed
like a gift from the skies. They couldn't have been
more excited if we'd come across a couple of stray
Catholics. They were all for loosing off our total
reserves then and there. But I held them off. I had my
own strategy for this.

Maggie Leyland was always spoken of as a love-
child. And although this is only another word for
bastard, there is a difference in approach. When the
Playground used such a term, it was forgetting its
respectability and showing its respect.

I did not know what it was about Maggie Leyland's
mum that made everyone respect her. Perhaps it was
because she never behaved as if she had anything to
be ashamed of. But that cannot have been the whole
story, because then they would have called her
shameless, which was one of the worst things they
knew how to say about anyone. My mam and my nan

were never anything but ashamed of me. They pushed it so far that they ended up by having good reason to be.

No. It wasn't a question of shame. The Leylands had a touch of quality. That was the Playground's rarest and most meaningful bit of praise. They couldn't have said what it meant.

The thing that struck me first about Maggie Leyland and her mum was how alike they were. You seldom saw them out of doors, except together: Maggie holding on to her mum's arm, and yet always contriving to be half a step behind her. They had the same face, the same uncommonly vaulted forehead, the same mouse-dun hair, the same curved nose. Maggie and I had started school together, and we were in the same class until we moved up out of the infants, after which we did not see much of each other—she was not allowed out on the Playground alone. But we met sometimes, if I was out shopping with my mam, and she stopped to talk to Maggie's mum. Maggie and I would stand there, looking at each other, neither of us saying a word. Maggie had a shy and penetrating way of looking at me—a way of looking at me that she never did seem to lose.

And there they were on Bonfire Night, their flanks unguarded, behind them a great, dark void, in which I could deploy my support troops as I wished. It was no time for crudity; it called for tactical genius. After a lot of whispering to my three silly sods, we had a semi-circle of bangers planted in the soil behind the Leyland pair: not farting little squibs, but plutocratic twopenny "cannons," that I had been saving for people's letterboxes. They had to be simultaneous.

The touch-papers all had to be lit at the same moment.

The curious thing is that I was certain that Maggie Leyland knew all along that we were there, and what we were up to. Once or twice she looked over her shoulder and tightened her grip on her mother's arm. But she said nothing to her mum; just braced herself for the shock. I think Maggie Leyland would have bought her way on to the Playground at any price.

I got the idea then—and God knows it's been reinforced since—that Maggie Leyland wanted to be shocked. She wanted to be one of us, even at our price, and always seemed ready to help to prepare the ground for whatever shit's trick I was going to play on her next.

Even after we were married.

The WPC who brought Kenworthy's coffee wore her uniform with a hint of jauntiness. It suggested that in the field, unharassed by immediate supervision, she might be capable of a certain down-to-earth initiative. But she seemed to think it appropriate to treat Kenworthy as a demure and well briefed niece might handle an unfamiliar uncle. Kenworthy slipped with natural graciousness into the allotted role.

"I'm just reading about Mrs. Bielby. You, of course, must have known the lady."

"I met her several times, sir—when last she was mayoress. Though of course, that's a few years now, and she hasn't shown herself at functions a good deal since. Rather a retiring lady; but popular with people at one time."

"At one time?"

"What I mean is, sir, that people forget. She's been out of the public eye for a long time."

"A good match for Bielby, you'd think?"

"I'd say definitely not, sir. Though he's supposed to have been very fond of her at one time."

"At one time. There we go again."

"What I'm trying to say, sir, is that it didn't come as any surprise to Filton-in-Leckerfield that Bielby had been playing away from home. But there are a lot of folk around who still won't believe that his wife was up to anything."

Kenworthy nodded vacantly and returned to Bielby's script.

• 3 •

THERE WERE TWO types of people to whom the Depression did not make much measurable difference: there were those who'd never been any better off anyway; and there were those who weren't geared to production. It was the first time in living memory that there hadn't been a token stir of smoke from the chimneys of the Prince Consort.

We never quite hit the bottom, my mam, my nan and I. My nan had her war widow's pension; my mam had five shillings a week on an affiliation order for me. And they both went out charring, at places that still had to be kept clean; my nan at the Gas Showrooms, where they still had work on hand, cutting off people's cookers, and seeing if people had broken into their meters; and my mam at a bank, where they hadn't got all the tradespeople's overdrafts in yet.

We had a greengrocer whom we called Noddy because his head kept bobbing up and down like an egg-bound pullet's, especially when he was weighing something. Once he sold my mam some onions that were rotten through to the middle, and she winked at me next time she went, and helped herself to compensation while his back was turned. Noddy was a preacher on a Free Church circuit, and saved his good works for that side of his life. He and the Town Moor kept an eye on each other, but there was one side of the balance-sheet on which he always lost out: the Town Moor never prayed for him.

Noddy's pomegranates were the first new line that I introduced to a wider public than he had intended. We'd seen them in his window and argued with each other about what they were. Then we talked in a vague way about how we could organize ourselves a sample. But I had great difficulty in recruiting a task force, and in the end I had to get the Bennetts and the Stringers in on the job, which in itself was a minor triumph. They were older than me, had already left school, and had had more than one brush with the law. They thought I was too young for their dignity, and I could not get them to see that they needed my brains. In the end, I got them through their sense of bravado.

It was Noddy's lamp that was our first concern. We called it Noddy's lamp because it stood outside his shop and he left his bedroom curtains open to undress by the light at night. I could be nimble if there was anything in it for me, even though games as such did not interest me at school. I soon shinned up that lamp and had it out.

And then the street was shrouded in an uncanny quiet. I'd never seen it at that time of night without a light on. There were one or two other shops in the row, but none of them was much more than a converted front room, and the people lived in the back parts of their houses. The asphalt was uneven under-foot, where it had been torn up again and again for work on the mains and sewers. I can't say I wasn't nervous.

We'd only one bobby to worry about, old Brewster, and he was my next responsibility. I knew his beat, and it was a matter of keeping him out of earshot while the Stringers deployed brute force on Noddy's roll-up shutter. I found my job easy enough. A scamper of heels was enough to get Brewster round a corner. I crouched behind a dustbin and lobbed an old tin into a yard in another street. Constable Brewster didn't see it go up, but he heard it come down. I moved round the next corner and decoyed him behind a row of distant closets. He set up a cat, which got among somebody's milk bottles, thereby doing a lot of my work for me. Brewster, moving steadily further away from Noddy's, thought he had got his quarry well pinned down by now. I heard him curse when he barked his shins against a wall.

I'll say this for the Stringers and the Bennetts: there was enough fresh fruit knocking about Swallow Street in the next day or two to stand between the Town Moor and a scurvy epidemic. Old Mosley had some; so did the Simpsons. But I didn't give any to my mam and nan in case they shopped me for it.

It was about this time that old Mosley threw his hand in. He had silicosis and pneumoconiosis, and several other things that are to be got in coal mines, which he summed up as "the dust," spitting on anything that happened to be handy, coal for prefer-ence. He had things neatly measured out. They found a spoonful of peas in his inside at the post-mortem.

I did several other jobs with the Stringers after
Noddy's: a market lorry, while the dealer, desperately
short-handed, was setting up stall one Saturday morning; Tunnicliffes'; a Co-op delivery van parked overnight. But I never would join in anything to do with
Harry Lester's fish and chip shop.

This piece of protection originated in mixed moral-
ity. I was already milking Harry of enough to keep me
in Woodbines. I'd happened to be in his place one
deserted evening halfway between paydays, and we'd
both seen a bloody great rat run across from the back
room where he chopped his chips to the cupboard
where he kept the flour for his batter. Harry was up
after it, the rat jumped up in the air, and Harry took it
a full toss with his fire-shovel, a hell of a *Whang!*
straight over the counter into his boiling fat pan.

"Say nowt!" Harry said. And he gave me a
shilling.

After that, I'd only to put my head round his door
and say, "How about that rat, Harry?" and he'd slip
me a threepenny bit or a tanner. And I had the sense
not to overdo it. He could have faced me out over that
rat, if he'd wanted to.

I was a fair thorn in the flesh of those two women
at about this time. And the typical end-of-term report
I was getting from school was "Easily satisfied—
Capable but indolent—Plays to the gallery—Wasting
his time and mine." I'd won a scholarship to the
Grammar School, which I didn't want—about the
only thing I'd ever agreed with my nan about. But by
nagging me into blisters my mam got me there.

It was a move that nearly buggered up my standing
on the Playground. At the very beginning, homework

tended to keep me off the shale during the fruitiest part of the evening; but I soon found better ways of doing it—including not doing it at all. In any case my mam and my nan soon got tired of keeping a corner of the table cleared for French and physics books. There were some things, like the sauce and the milk bottle, that they saw no point in putting away between meals.

It's an odd thing that it should have been Maggie's mum who seemed to set the fashion for belated marriages. There were a few desultory jokes about it, round the Playground; it made a change from Princess Marina and Mae West. But for the first time in my life I had little taste for smut. Mrs. Leyland was different.

We all went to the wedding. Even Sonny Simpson and his mother were waiting outside the railings, Sonny cow-eyed and blubber-mouthed in a suit that did not fit him. It was my first experience of the marriage service, and, cynic though I thought myself, I was impressed. The organ voluntary—*Because*—made my eyes begin to smart. I was moved by the March from *Lohengrin*. I was moved by the sight of Mrs. Leyland in a dove-grey two-piece. I even approved of the loving way in which she looked at the little cove she was marrying.

The whole Playground was bomb-happy for her. And I looked more than twice at Maggie, too; also in a dove-grey costume, the facial resemblance to her mum even stronger than ever. But Maggie was growing up. I was not much of a connoisseur of sexual appurtenances in those days, but I got the general picture. She looked more like a being in her own right than I had ever seen her before. The thought struck me that she was much nearer to being a woman than I was to being a man.

Afterwards there were sausage rolls, ham and tongue sandwiches, and wedding cake with coloured cachous that tasted of scent. It's a pity they hadn't submitted their shopping list to me and the Stringers. We could have saved them a penny or two.

Then I found that Maggie was coming to our house to stay for a night or two while her mum and her new dad were sentimentalizing over seed-cake and gnat's piss tea in Southport. This had been kept closely secret from me; and God knows what I'd have cooked up for Maggie if I'd had time to give my mind to it.

She was going to have my bedroom and I was going to sleep downstairs on the settee. And this was a problem—not that I begrudged her my bed—but the upstairs window, in conjunction with the drainpipe, had become a regular route for me when the house had settled for the night. It wasn't that I went out every night, but I felt cooped up when the channel was blocked. I didn't like using downstairs doors and windows; it meant leaving them unfastened, and there were people about the Town Moor who were less than honest.

We came away from the party before Maggie did, and I got under the women's feet at home, so my mam asked why didn't I go for a walk. So I did, and I slipped down to Unthank's to buy one of their practical jokes—actually *bought* it—and when Maggie arrived, we sat round the fire and listened to *In Town Tonight* and *Music Hall*. And I sat out of the line of vision of the two women and stuck an imitation nose-drop up one nostril. It was a horrible thing, like a big glass bubble, with a trickle that ran down like candle-fat over my upper lip. I could see that Maggie was tickled—nothing ever happened to her; and my reputation about the Playground had now grown so monstrous that I knew she was expecting big things from me in the next day or two.

But the shine was soon knocked off the evening. The compère had just announced Stainless Stephen when someone hammered at the door, and it was a couple of characters who made our living room look suddenly small. One was PC Brewster and the other a detective-constable in plain clothes.

"It's your lad we wanted a word with."

My nan gave me a look that said she was in no way surprised, and she'd get even with me later for landing them with this in front of Maggie. She had a great patch of alopecia, a shining bald knob on the crown of her head like the arse of a feather-pecked chicken, and in profile she looked like something out of a Punch and Judy show. She had a hooked nose and an upturned chin and I remember thinking that one of these days they'd grow together, and she'd have to work her fork sideways to get food into her mouth.

And my mam was walking up and down, twisting and untwisting her fingers.

"What have you been doing, our Sidney?"

"Nothing."

"Do you want me to come with you, then, love?"

"I can manage."

I did not want her with me, but I had to put it as casually as I could. I didn't know what was on, but I knew she would bugger up whatever chance I had of talking my way out of it. I guessed that the coppers did not want her, either. But then my nan started going for her coat.

"Well, I'll go with him, if his own mother won't."

And *Sod that!* I thought. And all the time, Maggie was trying to look so absorbed in the radio that she wasn't taking in any of our private affairs. And my brain was working like a cement mixer, wondering what they'd found out, and how I was going to keep the old woman out of it. I knew one thing for certain: if my nan came with me, I was finished: she'd have perjured herself to see me further up the creek than I was already.

I needn't have worried. It was bluff and counter-bluff. Neither of them wanted the disturbance, and I was taken across town to the police station, and upstairs to a room where they hadn't even gone to the expense of a floor-covering: just a dirty grey wooden floor, with a trestle table loaded with piles of papers in tatty folders. Junk had to be moved off the chairs before anybody could sit down. And they hadn't had me up there more than a minute or two when I began to think I ought to have let my mam come after all. Brewster caught me one across the ear with a hand like a number seven shovel, and when I cringed away the other bastard came up with his knuckles into the fleshy part of my arm.

Old Crowther pitched into me from the Bench and ordered me six strokes of the birch. I won't say it didn't hurt, but even in those days I was working to a system that had never failed me. I can stand most things if I mark out the halfway spot in my mind first, and then start telling myself that I'm on the home stretch. I gritted my teeth for the first three, and when it was finished, it was finished.

But I still felt worked up by some of the things that they'd charged me with. There were nine offences on the sheet, and I'd been concerned in four of them. And they hadn't found out about the things they could really have sent me sailing for. It was the Bennetts who'd shopped the Stringers and the Stringers who'd shopped me. There's a lot of talk about honour among thieves, but that must be when you get up among the higher echelons. What riled me most was that they had me down for doing Armitage's. My mam had to stop shopping there—and she never did square with him for the last nine pennyworth she'd had.

Birching did me neither good nor harm. Perhaps it was good for the sergeant who laid it on; he might have gone across the yard, otherwise, and taken it out on a lost dog. But I remember the crowd round me in the Playground afterwards, wanting to know what it was like. And I remember the special stool they used for me to bend over—rather like the base of a cottage spinning-wheel—and how there'd been another copper standing at the side, counting the shots aloud, as if they weren't certain that the other old sod could manage up to six for himself. I didn't show my arse to everybody on the Playground; only to the inner circle. And I didn't charge for it, a penny a look, as Albert Boardman did when he'd had it.

I was expelled from the Grammar School. They could do that to you in those days. Old Bundy was the headmaster, R. Charlton Bundy, Esq., M.A., and he gave me six more for bringing the name of the school into disrepute. I remember how I stood looking at him until his face and his bald head seemed to grow so big that I could see nothing else. And I remember looking at his lower front teeth, and thinking how absurdly small they were, like a rabbit's. What a stupid bugger he must be, to have piddling little teeth like that! It was over a quarter of a century before I was to walk back into his study. Bundy was on the verge of retirement then, and I had got myself elected, just in time, to his Board of Governors. The first thing I looked at was his front teeth, but there seemed nothing abnormal about them.

Something was happening between my mam and my nan at this time. I'd grown up with their running warfare, and I didn't think there could be anything new under that sun. In fact, until this new wave swept up, there was hardly any steam left in their hostility. They twitched and snivelled like a pair of bitches ratting in their sleep.

Now something new was going on. They had never offered each other physical violence, but it began to look as if something was going to snap. They stopped speaking to each other and, unbelievably, their silence was more ominous than their verbal skirmishing. They moved out of each other's way at the cooker. They started playing at being polite; and that was the most lethal thing of all.

This was an empty stretch in my life. I didn't get up in the morning until the women had gone out to their charing. And with no school to go to, it would often be half past ten before I came downstairs half-dressed. For the rest of the day I hung about the Playground. It stands to sense that if there was no work for me, there was none for an under-age criminal. One of the Stringers had been sent to Borstal; one of the Bennetts to an Industrial School. I had no friends. I hadn't a penny in my pocket. I hadn't saved any money; I wasn't earning any; I wasn't at the moment stealing any, and I wasn't given any. Even Harry Lester's rat had stopped paying up. I didn't play games, not even in fantasy. I hadn't the spirit, and I wasn't a kid any more. And the men—there were plenty of them hanging about the shale in 1933— didn't want my company.

I talked to no one. The unemployed had almost given up talking to each other. They'd sit round in little circles on their haunches, and if there was a dog-end between a group, they'd pass it round from mouth to mouth. They could have gone fishing in the canal—and when they'd been in work, it hadn't been past some of them to play hookey on the tow-path. But now there wasn't even a stolen apple taste about that.

And I kept hearing things at home that suggested something in the offing. One of these days, something was going to happen. Even the word "happen" had an unrealistic ring about it on the Playground at that time.

"Well, if you haven't learned one lesson in your life," my nan said to my mam, "I suppose you'll not rest until you've learned another. And who's going to look after me, that's what I want to know? I'm damned if I'd want to be second mate to that damned shyster."

I saw my mam's forearm twitch and I moved out of the immediate danger area. But they did not actually come to blows. A day or two later, my mam put on a desperate act of trying to get me on my own, wearing a look that said bygones were bygones; she needed an ally. I made things as difficult for her as I could, but she cornered me in the end.

"Sid—how would you like to leave Filton?"

I turned the wireless up. It was Henry Hall, and Len Bermon was singing *She Wore a Little Jacket of Blue*. My mam came over and switched the set off. Out on the Playground there was a steady drizzle. I went out, all the same.

The next day, she got me alone again. She had a drop of petrol in an old bottle, and was trying to get a grease spot out of a pair of my old flannels.

"Sidney—you're coming with me on Saturday. And you'll not bloody let me down. If you've never done anything for me in your life before, and you never do anything again—I'll make it up to you, Sid. Honest to Christ I will. God knows you've never had a chance, not on this crap heap."

She started to cry, which made me less sympathetic than ever. Women can look damned ugly when they're crying.

"It's only to Blackpool," she said, "and you'll have most of the time to yourself. I'll see you have money in your pocket."

She offered me five shillings—half a crown before we started, the rest after I'd shaken hands with Arthur Bielby without buggering things up for her. I had to resign myself to not messing up her chances.

Arthur Bielby was to come on the afternoon train from London. We were there a couple of hours before him, but my mam would not let me go out until I was on the right side of that handshake. She wouldn't even let me out on the clifftop to see what the tide was doing. And I didn't go much for the residents' lounge, with dust deep in the upholstery, and a marble clock fifty years slow. My mam had built up a bit of drama for the reunion, but it did not come to much. Arthur Bielby had carried his case up from Ginn Square, and wanted nothing more than to put it down and flex his fingers. And the landlady couldn't wait until he was fairly in the house before she recited her rules. So my mam had to hang about half in and half out of the lounge door, and wasn't able to make much capital out of the way she came through it. Then I had to be called from the wings for my walk-on part. Shaking hands with Arthur Bielby was rather like fingering the hindquarters of a dead but still warm rabbit.

There is more than one advantage about deciding to hate a man before you've ever set eyes on him. You've got him from the start, if you can be strong enough never to give an inch. One glance at him, in the hall of that boarding house, and I knew I was his master. He was bigger than the man Maggie's mum had married—a little. He wasn't quite as bald, he had a bit more breadth about his shoulders, and he had a pair of blue eyes that might possibly in their time have seen a joke. He tried to crack a few that weekend, but I made sure he didn't get a smile out of me.

I know now—and I knew then—that I was being less than fair to him. He was—except for the lapse that had brought me into being—a clean-living man; he worked hard; he was moderately thrifty without being mean. He liked his pint at the weekend, but he never got drunk. His first wife had just died after a long illness and he had nursed her at home with the

minimal help that was to be had in the thirties. He had
been through the mill and come creditably down the
chute. And God knows what he thought of my mam,
seeing her for the first time again after all those years.
He never showed anything but a sort of courteous
pride at being in her presence. When I saw them
together again, after the Second World War, I recognized genuine affection. Perhaps he was sincere that
afternoon in Blackpool; maybe he was only acting up
decent. I wasn't prepared to admit either possibility.

But I had to be a little circumspect, at least until I
was on the right side of my mam's second half-crown.
And he supplemented it with a ten-shilling note, for
which I did have the *savoir vivre* to mumble a
thank-you. Fifteen shillings was reasonable potential:
fish, chips, *Vimto* and the Golden Mile. It was a treat
to get out into the fresh air of the Promenade, and
there I ran into Top-Notch Randall, with whom I took
a turn both ways along the seafront.

Top-Notch drove a tram in Filton. He used to live
near us at that time. When few other people had work
to do, we could hear Top-Notch's clog irons on the
pavement in the early hours of the morning, and we
could picture him in his peaked cap and big ragged
gloves, his breath steaming in the frost.

They called him Top-Notch because it was a point
of honour with him never to drive his tram with the
power less than full on, even if he was only backing
down a couple of yards at the terminus. Many a new
conductor had had to cling to the platform like a
coxswain to a lifeboat. And when a copper on point
duty tried to hold him up, he'd come clanging up at a
rate of knots and then stop dead, with less than a foot

to spare in front of the tunic buttons. The funny thing
was that he always got away with it. Two or three
times a week he did something that anybody else
would have got the sack for.

Top-Notch had a set of standards of his own. Take
me, for example, crossing the tramlines on the South
Shore, excited to spot a familiar figure as far from
home as that. My name was pit-slurry on the Town
Moor. It hadn't been in the *Examiner*; but they didn't
need newspapers in Elgin Row. They might have
forgiven me for doing anybody but old Armitage.
And seeing me across the road, anybody put Top-
Notch would have developed a sudden interest in
something distant.

Top-Notch was a Quaker or something. He used to
disappear to Bolton on Sunday mornings, because
there were others of his lot there. I don't know
whether he rated as a good Quaker or not; but you can
be certain that he wasn't a characteristic one. Put him
in a minority, and he'd found another of his own
inside it. You always got the impression that whatever
code he answered to was something that no one else
had thought of yet. Perhaps that had something to do
with why they never threw him off the trams. Though
mostly, I think, that was because of his dry wit. Even
when the inspectors ticked him off, it was only
because they wanted to hear his back talk. His
conductors always used to complain that they saw
more inspectors than anybody else did; but they only
got on for the laugh. He pulled up once not half a yard
from the Mayor's November church procession, spinning his brake handle like a roulette wheel, clanging
his bell to be let through the middle of the Town

Council, craggy old bugger that he was, with a chin like a snow plough. The vermin in ermine got more fun out of that than they did out of the Chaplain's sermon, that's a certainty. He looked on his tram as a sort of biblical chariot that he was hurling against the grime of Filton and its veneer of pomp.

"Nah, Top-Notch."

"Nah, Sid."

"Gradely afternoon."

"It is that, lad."

He looked out towards the sea. You could see the blur up north of the Furness hills, behind the curve of Morecambe Bay.

"I allus come here on me day off," he said. "There's summat about t' watter."

"Aye."

"Art going up Tower, then?"

"Ah don't think ah will. It costs too much."

You could say that to Top-Notch without it sounding like a touch.

"It does that. Ah'd rather smell yon watter than them moth-eaten lions. At least 'tis human sewage as is floating out there."

"Ah wonder tha doesna get a job on one o' these trams here."

"Nay, Sid. Wheer should ah go on day off, if ah were to do that?"

He never asked questions. He waited for people to tell him things. And when you spoke to him, he often wouldn't answer right away. He'd be silent for several seconds, as if he thought that anything at all that anybody said was well worth weighing up.

"Me mam's thinking of getting wed," I said, not

because I had any such positive information as, I suppose, out of an innate sense of mischief-making. And anybody else from the Town Moor would have showered me with questions. But Top-Notch went through his routine of silence. It gave the impression that he knew a great deal more than was possible about what was going on. Certainly he could see pretty deeply into me. Top-Notch always did give me an uncomfortable feeling about myself.

"Tha knows," he said at last. "Ah wor on trams when they wor still pulled be 'orses. Now they're talking about finishing wi' trams for good and all."

"What'll tha do then, Top-Notch?"

"Ah s'll worry about it when it 'appens. Ah didna know what ah wor going to do when they send owd Tinker to t' knacker."

The first day he had taken his electric tram out of the shed, he had pushed the power-handle hard over. It had been there since. It was some sort of gesture.

I was reluctant to go back to the boarding house, and that was not entirely due to bloody-mindedness. I did not know how to deal with my embarrassment. I could not be at ease when my mam and Arthur Bielby were together. And the lounge was full of strangers: men with their shirt collars open and old women in drab heavy frocks, and they were all as hushed as if they were studying a pit-head casualty list. There was a big old wireless set in a corner and they were listening to the Kentucky Minstrels singing Doris Arnold's arrangement of *The Lost Chord*. A sanctimonious old bastard from Chadderton told me to "Sh!" before I was fairly into the room.

And I caught sight of my mam's hand dangling

over the arm of her chair, and Arthur Bielby was letting his finger tips brush against her knuckles. so I crept up to bed, but later, when I got up to the loo, she came and waylaid me on the landing.

"He's your dad," she whispered, so conspiratorial that I wanted to fetch up. Then she said, "Your dad and I are going to get married," and I saw the funny side of that and laughed, and she caught me one across my face that knocked the breath out of me.

"That's for trying to ruin my bloody life for me. Well, you can take your pick. You can come and live with us in Essex, or you can stay in Filton with your nan. But if you come with us, there have got to be a few understandings. I've had all the misery I need for a lifetime, and I'm taking no more of it from you."

I knew she meant it. And I knew there were ears pressed up against the panels of bedroom doors, listening to us. In fact, the man from Chadderton came out of one of them, in his vest, with his braces dangling, and went down the half flight of stairs to the bog. We heard him piss, and he missed the pan, and we could hear it pattering on the lino. And my mam and I both laughed. It was funny; a bloke we didn't know couldn't aim straight, and the moment brought us together.

"Try and like your father, Sid," she said.

And I said, "Aye," but the moment was over and I had to get away from her. I thought it out in bed. I certainly wasn't going to suck up to Arthur Bielby, but it was playing safe to go and see what Essex was like. The way my mam pronounced the word over the next few weeks, you'd have thought it was the Promised Land. To me it meant I was getting my fare paid to put two hundred miles between me and my nan. That made it worthwhile not actually insulting Arthur Bielby to his face.

We went to church next morning, and it was all fixed for him to get me to himself on our way back.

"Your mum," he said—he couldn't even get that right—"wants to go and look in the dress shop windows. Let's have a little blow along the front."

I made it difficult for him to stay in step with me. And then he started cracking up Essex, how I'd like Felixstowe and Clacton better than this coast. And he'd see to it that I'd be able to finish my schooling, and it would be easier for me, because no one knew me down there. I'd make decent friends. Did I play cricket? He'd teach me to bowl slow off-spinners. And of course he'd see that I got a job. Just as soon as I got my *Mat*ric—he pronounced it in a weird way, with the accent on the first syllable. There was magic in *Mat*ric.

Arthur Bielby was a printer by trade, had risen from apprenticeship to be senior compositor at Busby's. He seemed to think that Busby's was a name to juggle with, even up here. He'd have no difficulty in getting me taken on. After I'd got my *Mat*ric. Unless, of course, I wanted to be something other than a printer. He wasn't going to force me into something that I didn't want. (Too bloody true he wasn't!) Arthur Bielby was essentially a simple man, and he saw things simply. He saw that something was "for the best" and saw no sense in deviating from course thereafter. He was an easy man to hate. There was nothing quite so hateful as his bloody decency.

That evening I went into a pub, but was so blatantly

underage that they saw me off without dignity. So I went and watched the sunset on the sea: gold, green and turquoise. A smudge of steamer smoke; a swell of variegated colour where the waves combed over a sand bank. I was quite unexpectedly impressed. We were a bit short of skylines on the Town Moor.

Kenworthy paid a visit to the officers' urinal, and under that cover managed to slip out of the station without the incubus of a pilot. He made his way to that spot on the magpie ring between Filton's inner and outer circles that still went under the name of the Town Moor.

He hardly expected to see the roll-front of Noddy's green grocery, but he had hoped to find some recognizable relic of Swallow Street or Colliery Street or Elgin Row, perhaps half a street in red Accrington brick, still lived in for the dying space of a condemnation order. But it had all gone. Where he judged the grey slag of the goal to have been, stood the extensive walls, so far empty, of a new shopping complex. Aerosol graffiti sprawled over half-finished walls that would shortly house the predictable run of Card Shops, Wine Stores and Television Rentals.

Shortly? There was a stillborn air about the site. Vandalism, not all that recent, had gone unattended along the draughty arcades: here a barricade was stove in, there a wiring circuit ripped hilariously through the plaster board. There was a large placard, target for a variety of missiles, including excrement, advertising valuable trading properties to rent, and inviting enquiries to a London address. But the frames that had carried the names of subcontractors were all vacant. There was not even evidence of a main contractor, and a wooden hut that might have housed a clerk of works was minus glazing, door and half its roof.

• 4 •

I FOUND THINGS to like, in spite of myself, in Essex, but they were not, it goes without saying, of Bielby provision: a cinema with a Wurlitzer organ, electricians' shops stocked with all mains radios. The south of England was pulling out of the Depression more resiliently than the north. There was evidence here of the things that money could buy.

Of course my parents (not that I ever realistically thought of Arthur Bielby as a parent) sickened me. Their sex life was so furtive that it became blatant. But then I'd never moved about with anyone who hadn't looked on sex as furtive. The kids were furtive about their experiments. Mothers and fathers, past experiment, were furtive behind their flimsy bedroom walls. We were even furtive about the extent of our knowledge, concealing from our elders our acquaintance—extensive, perverted and frequently fallacious—with the facts of life. It was about the only courtesy we paid to their seniority.

In Essex, I'd even lost my identity. I wasn't even Sid Wheeler any more. I was Roger Bielby. Roger was my second name, which I'd always done my best to keep dark in Filton. And Bielby—! They reasoned with me about the common sense of being known by the same handle as your father—especially when he *was* your father—but I remained unconvinced. Why the hell hadn't they christened me Goal-mouth?

And I lost the battle to keep out of school: lost it despite a campaign of temperamental terrorism that must have threatened to break up the new partnership. On my way across the new playground on the first morning, I was tempted to turn back and lose myself in the parks and side streets. The moment I passed through the unfamiliar cloakroom, I knew I was trapped. I became a member of the least academic and least industrious of fifth forms, and this depressed community, with its shoddy blazers and its Londonized East Anglian diphthongs, was unwilling to open its ranks to a newcomer. The only way in which I knew how to appeal to them was through the ingenuity and monstrous impudence of my idleness. Until I was suddenly pushed in the opposite direction by a lizard of a man who taught us history.

Harrison had a bludgeoning line in sarcasm which he did not rest for a minute of his day. It happened that he casually asked me the dates of the Crimean War and I, half-slumbering, too lethargic even to shrug him off, said "1853 to 1856." (I don't know how I knew.)

Harrison put on a wild act. He made me say it again. He made me go up and write the figures on the blackboard. He went round the room and shouted them into the ears of one boy after another.

"And Bielby knew!" he said. "Bielby knew! but how could Bielby possibly know? What secret charm can place-names like Inkerman and Balaclava possibly have for a pair of ears like Bielby's? Can it be that Bielby is actually fixing his sights on the distant pearly gates of Matriculation? Next year will he learn another couple of dates? And another, perhaps, the year after that? Don't overdo it, lad. Don't overstretch yourself. Would you like to go for a walk round the field until you feel yourself again?"

That decided me. I started working then as single-mindedly as I had once applied myself to Noddy's pomegranates. But it was all in secret. I decided I would owe nothing to the system. If I did any homework, I didn't hand it in—or else handed in something so slipshod that I remained above suspicion. To maintain my image, I deliberately cheated in a school examination; and equally deliberately allowed myself to be found out. Bartlett, the Old Man, brought his cane out of a curtained cupboard, rolled it on his table as if he were testing a billiard cue, and gave me six that I can still feel when I think about it. I thought the bugger was going to cut me in two.

But I stuck to it. Intellectually, it was no great trial. I had some feeling for mathematics: congruent triangles and corollaries to Appollonius. I had an almost photographic memory: the properties of halogens, the terms of treaties. I liked physics: Wheatstone's bridge and Nicholson's hydrometer. I made up mnemonics about Arkwright and Turnip Townshend.

My resulting *Mat*ric shattered them all. I only got one distinction (physics) but then I'd had a prohibitive fight against time. There was a sudden emetic whip-up of superlatives. I was suddenly credited with exceptional imagination. I was a Trojan; I had achieved a miracle of self-redemption. You'd have thought I'd done it all for their bloody sakes. And then, of course, the bastards started talking in terms of more school: technical college, perhaps university.

I had to go and see old Bartlett during that summer holiday, and the school had a deserted look that extended even to his study. He was wearing a pullover without a jacket. His secretary had just brought him a cup of coffee, and he made her bring me one. He made no reference to his assault on my flesh, and I tried not to let my eyes stray in the direction of the green-curtained cupboard. He made only a nominal attempt to make me stay on in the sixth form, and accepted my strenuous refusal with a smile.

"I think you're right, Bielby. Though I'd have liked your type of individualist with us for another couple of years. Maybe you'd be better off trying for independence. But what are you going to do?"

I did not know. I could have reeled off for him— they were familiar enough with it at home—an exhaustive list of all the sound and solid occupations that I would not touch. He rummaged amongst his papers and brought out a letter.

"There's a job here," he said, "that demands a rare combination of the thick-skinned and the sensitive. I'm surprised your father hasn't mentioned it to you."

It was written on the notepaper of the *Herald*, one of the papers that Arthur Bielby printed. They wanted a trainee reporter, and said there were opportunities for advancement. I knew why old Bielby had not told me about it. He knew what sort of reception he'd get if he suggested anything connected with Busby's.

"I'd like that," I said.

And I got it. Arthur Bielby, when he recovered from the body blow, was quietly satisfied. It started a new phase in our relationship. It did not make us friends, but without formal discussion of terms we became non-belligerents.

I have kept to this day an old copy of the *Herald* in which I marked with coloured pencil all the items with which I had some connection: a chimney fire on a council estate; a youth who had caught an old woman up the jacksie with an air rifle pellet; court cases—bastardy, bicycle lamps and nuisances in shop doorways. When someone's hen house was broken into, I was there, invited in for a cup of tea, the link with the real glory, able to turn the loss of a couple of Rhode Island Reds into the fame of newsprint. Whatever was locally on offer in the way of life, squalor or disaster, I was there, the link-man between the deed and its immortality.

All this took me through to the outbreak of war, which came as a massive relief from the personal problems that I had been accumulating. I was still only getting three pounds a week and owed more in advances up and down the office than I ever had hope of repaying. I was playing off three or four girls one against the other, and at least two of them suspected it. Yet another was trying to pull a pregnancy on me: a false alarm, as it happened, but feasible. I was an early volunteer for aircrew.

I don't mean to write much about the war. Other books about the RAF have said most of it. But the war did happen. I was of the age for it. And nothing bigger ever came my way. Did it broaden my horizons? Well, it got me to South Africa for training.

There was lavish hospitality in homes, the like of which I had not seen outside the cinema. There was a welcome from people who had everything done for them by servants, and whose territorial possessions made the English shires look like backyards. They spoke in a language of sentimental patriotism of a sort that it would have embarrassed us to mouth, but that made us feel that our existence was good.

Did the service make a man of me? I learned to drink like a buccaneer: eleven-a-side drinking matches in the mess; chess with pints on the chequered floor of a pub. We learned to take death in our stride: *"We planted Barry last Friday. Christ, he was a heavy bastard!"*

When I signed on, I had had no realistic thoughts about a commission. Officer rank was largely a matter of social stratum—they bought branded products—but it showed up more in the RAF because there were mixed ranks doing the same job. Pilot was skipper, and he could be a flight sergeant, overruling a flight lieutenant in the navigator's seat. It did not often work like that—they tried to see it didn't—but it could. There were a lot of us with similar qualifications and responsibility, only a handful sorted out to wear a different kind of cap, uniform of better quality cloth, better pay and allowances, better living conditions and a better chance with the women.

In my first few weeks, I didn't give it much thought. When it came to bullshit in the Initial Training Wing, I didn't try unduly hard. It didn't seem to me I'd get a better fix on a target for being able to shave in the toe caps of my boots. I shone them, certainly: I meant to pass. But I'd no wish to outdo the next man. I saw the types who were earmarked for rings round their cuffs, and they were mostly ex-public school prefects.

Then, walking back alone from cinema to camp one night, thinking about nothing extraordinary, I suddenly saw that if I could cross that gap now, I was across it for life. But I knew what was against me: my Lancashire speech, my ignoble Essex grammar school; a court conviction. There was no way of wiping that out. A man with a criminal record couldn't supervise the running up of the flag at reveille. Three lines of Air Ministry reference from R. Charlton Bundy, Esq., and I would be staying in the ranks.

I went back to Essex on a short leave, and I dropped in at school. They were running their own Air Cadets now, and old Bartlett was a sort of amateur squadron leader. I was tentative about trying for promotion; he was enthusiastic, and mentioned a few names of boys who had made the grade.

"Yes, sir. But I did get into trouble in Lancashire. They're bound to check up at my old school."

"That's all right. I'll write to Bundy."

"He'll never support me, sir. Not Mr. R. Charlton Bundy."

"He will when he's heard from me."

So I started boning my boots. It dawned on me that my blancoed belt and my Bluebelled brass were the only things about me that anyone saw or knew. It was like taking *Mat*ric all over again: except that this time I didn't bother to hide my intentions. I began to be looked on as an ambitious shit. Why dissimulate? I won a baton of honour for foot drill at the ITW. I took third place in the squadron for navigational theory. I was gazetted Pilot-Officer Bielby. One day I put a Chiefy on a charge for sloppy turnout.

I suppose I went the way of most converts. I didn't hoist myself up in the Establishment without coming to believe in it. I was an orthodox PO, living by the book because the book worked. I had no twinge of conscience about becoming a martinet: if an LAC skimped checking a circuit after a night on the batter, that kite might never come home.

Did I make any friends? None that abided. I have come to the conclusion that if a man in a lifetime makes half a dozen friends—real friends—he has not done so badly. There were men that I drank with. There were kites that I looked for when they flew home late and severally. When Archie Newsome tried to set fire to the North Sea, I drank double for single for a week. That may have been because it was rather a satisfying role to be playing.

Women? Sex? From one woman, on one 'drome, I learned what a man needs to know—and that he's lucky if he's ever taught.

It goes without saying that I'd had no experience at Filton-in-Leckerfield. I was still too young for it—though perhaps only by a matter of weeks. If we had stayed much longer, I would undoubtedly have found a taker, and learned the Playground way. It wasn't such a bad school, provided you didn't put someone up the spout and find yourself hobbled at eighteen. You couldn't shag yourself silly round the shooting-in goal without at least acquiring some sense of timing.

I learned on an Essex Recreation Ground. The Rec: a public garden, as phoney as the rest of the town;

pretentious, without the power to impress; leggy wallflowers, spattered with the Outer London clay. The Rec: Nellie Bradshaw. She gave a lot of men their first start in life. It would give a wrong impression to point too precise a comparison between Nellie Bradshaw and Sonny Simpson. If she'd had Sonny's eyes and jowls, she'd have had to whistle for customers. Let's say, she nearly had. But like Sonny, she was single-minded. Give Sonny a cauldron of sump oil, and woe betide the Catholics; Nellie took her orders from her glandular secretions. I don't know how old she was. One of the things she shared with Sonny was perpetual youth—of a sort.

I met her after my shorthand evening class. I was a thin and long-legged specimen at the time. I'd had to let down the turn-ups of my trousers to get a few months more out of them, and they were already well above my ankles. Nellie didn't look too bad, at a distance. She had a warm smile, was reasonably upholstered and mobile; a bit flabby, but not revoltingly so.

And she was well organized. She took me to a hide-out under and amid a clump of tatty flowering currants. And she seemed impatient—obviously didn't expect the preliminaries that the book said you shouldn't overlook. She went about in a perpetual state of readiness but I, on the other hand, was of a mind to romanticize even such a situation as this. I wanted to linger over the thought that this was a real, live, flesh-and-blood woman that I'd got here, with life pulsing in her veins, soft down on her cheeks and my reflection in her eyes. What I got was my nostrils full of spearmint and the tender charm of her invitation, "Well, go on, put your cock in."

Which she largely did for me. But it was no good. I was beyond self-control. She was kind, held my face against her breast with the flat of her hand. But when I felt her wriggling about, and discovered that this was in order to unwrap another sliver of chewing gum, I realized that the romance was over. My love life stayed on a spiritual plane for some months after that, partly because my current girlfriends were as unpermissive a bunch as a man is ever likely to meet. They wanted kicks, but not in boots. I got some harmless amusement from stubbing my toes.

I was mostly a dropout during my time on Ops. I even dropped out of sex for months on end, something I've never found it all that difficult to do, after the first week or so, at certain periods in my life. Scarcely a month went by in the Squadron without a whip-round for someone's wedding, and the country hotels were doing steady business. But I was out on a side path. It wasn't that I had taken any decision to stand out of the general rush; it just happened that way. Until I met Sally Carver.

We were ripping up the Ruhr from a pastoral airfield in West Suffolk. She was one of a pack from the Women's Land Army who came on the back of a lorry to a station dance. She was a big girl, wore a touch a make-up, not much, off-blonde hairstyle aimed principally at saving herself trouble, broad smile, though her eyes did not join in on it at first acquaintance. We had a casual hop, and I'm not quite sure how we came to bother with each other after that. Even less do I know why I plunged into the expensive rarity of a rural taxi to take her eight miles round the dark lanes to the hutted camp where she lived. There were a couple of planks lying over the coiled barbed wire of the compound, sign of regular traffic. She took me to a cubicle at the end of one of the bunkhouses—an iron-framed hospital bed, with brown blankets, sagging in the middle. She had improvised an indoor clothesline from a length of coarse string, and the sight of her whipcord breeches hanging from it affected me more than all the legs in the Windmill. She did a bit of rapid tidying up as we got in, but neither of us was in much of a mood for waiting.

I made a better job of it than I had with Nellie Bradshaw—and thought I'd not done so badly for her, either. But after she'd smoked a cigarette and let me lie for a bit, she did not mince her words.

"That the best you can do?"

After that she took me in hand, over a period of eight or nine months. The postgraduate course was recherché stuff. What we liked about each other—we said—was our straight understanding that this was only make do and mend. She was married to a radio operator, a poor devil who was ferrying stuff across the Atlantic. And nobody was going to come between them. When Dave came back, if Dave came back, it was going to be "Eyes front!" for Sally Carver. But, as she said, good years were passing, and she didn't expect him to live like a monk in Boston and Newport.

Now and then I had to break a date to blow a few Germans out of their beds and bunkers, sometimes without notice. But I knew she could take this as it came—just as I had to, when Dave docked for a refit, and she disappeared in the direction of the Strand Palace. When she came back I always had to let it go for a week or two before she'd allow me near her. I had respect for Sally Carver.

Then one night I was briefed out of turn to skipper a scratch crew in a thousand-bomber saturation raid east of the Rhine—Oberhausen: my target was a steelworks. We'd seen it all before—except for a couple of pairs of greenish hands that I had in the turrets—a Brock's Benefit for Bonfire Night: purple chrysanthemums streaming up round us, marker flares ahead, floating down among the hanging smoke puffs. I never did skirt flak without remembering the Playground.

Of course I was scared. We were all bloody scared. Crew who weren't scared were no bloody good to me. They didn't know what it was about. I kidded myself that they knew they could trust me to keep my feelings to myself. They could panic, within reason, down the intercom, and they wouldn't get panic back. But they'd know when I wasn't kidding, when the voice might seem casual, but the words meant jump to it. All normal; that was how we got out and home again.

But tonight wasn't normal. I'd these two mixed infants. They'd been too excited at takeoff. They were likely to think, if a lump of shrapnel jagged through the fabric, that this was "it." We were rocking at airbursts. We'd lost contact with the rear gunner, didn't know whether his line was dead or he was. And we'd this bloody great bomb under us, big enough to have done for the whole of Filton-in-

Leckerfield; or us. I was jittery; operationally, we did not know each other.

Sally Carver had been back a week from Merseyside. Tonight we'd have met again for the first time. She might spot one of my regular crew in the local, and think I was up to something. It did not matter; it would come out in the wash. There was always tomorrow. But thinking too much about tomorrow, you got the feeling that today might not last.

We saw someone explode in midair. T—Tango disintegrated like a twopenny star shell against the Cephos poster. It had all happened before. We sidestepped in the blast-wave. A searchlight got us and held us. Four streams of tracer arced up and missed us. I took evasive action. Barely intelligible, someone else's invective came in over our radio-net. I swept up and away from our bombing run. We had got out of phase. A new wave was coming in behind us.

There was nothing original about jetisonning a bomb, but it was the first time I'd done it for reasons I wouldn't have told the IO about. I couldn't have stood another run-in on Oberhausen. I climbed way for two full minutes. Below was the black tumour of a residential area. I told the bomb aimer to let her go, and he started getting argumentative.

"We're losing height," I said, and the copilot turned quizzically. He knew that we weren't.

"Get rid!"

Relieved of our load, we shot up like a lift up a shaft. I pulled us into control. It seemed an age before anything happened. Perhaps there hadn't been a bomb at all, and we'd thrown a heavy nothing away; perhaps it was a dud. Then flame erupted.

Out of somewhere like Colliery Street, or Swallow
Street, or Elgin Row, or thirty, three hundred, three
thousand streets like them: chimney cowls and slates,
old Armitage's shop and Noddy's. Eight acres of
smoking rubble. I don't know where it was. I've
studied the map since and tried to work it out. I've
settled on Sternkragen, but it may have been
Hamborn—though I don't think we were as far over
as that.

We sliced the summit off another plume of shit and
dirt somewhere over Holland. I heard one of the struts
go, and an airburst all but had our port engine. And I
started seeing old Mosley again. Maybe one wave of
conscience recalls another. Maybe the image of Mosley meant death. I'd tried to describe it to Sally
Carver, but she was no more help than anyone else.
"Put him out of your mind," she said. "He'd have
done it whether you'd been there or not."

"I could have gone for help."

"So he'd have done it some other time."

"I went and fetched him his razor."

"He'd have gone and got it himself."

"I wanted him to do it. I wanted something to
happen."

We got back from Oberhausen with a fuel-feed
gone and the starboard flaps barely answering. There
seemed to be a hell of a lot of North Sea. We
hedge-hopped into Suffolk.

And it would make a neat tale to say that we came
in low over Sally Carver's field at dawn, skimming
Sally Carver's knot of huts. We didn't. No such
coincidence. But we came in over fields like it, and
similar camps. The dawn was grey, as if the skies

were running short on proper daylight. I had an unequivocal word in my crew's ears before we went for debriefing. And I never did see Sally Carver again. I kept out of her way. That is something about myself that I have never understood.

When I came out of the RAF I was suffering mildly from agoraphobia. At least, that's what I've always told myself. I'm not sure I really know what agoraphobia is, but it seems to me that the main comfort of medical science is finding neat labels. I call myself a mild case, because I managed never to have to report it. But it gave me some bad times, and I had to work my own way out of them, sometimes in funny places, like the top of a bus, or crossing a deserted road. It was a sort of vertigo, and I wanted to crawl into the nearest undergrowth—or the womb-like familiarity of something curiously like the hull of a Lancaster.

That was why, I suppose, contrary sod as always, after the briefest look at civilian life, I went back to flying.

Kenworthy screwed up a ball of paper and flicked it across the office floor with one of the putters from the bag that still leaned against the wall.

Odd thing: the club was too short for him, though he was pretty much the height that Bielby had been. Bartram was a shorter man.

Custom-built.

And at that moment the half-moon jowls and gooseberry eyes of the superintendent paid a courtesy call round the door, as they did every hour or so. An excellent host; or curiosity that would not keep?

Kenworthy returned the putter to the bag, saying

nothing about it. Bartram did not refer to it, either,
but let his eyes rest on Bielby's pages on the desk.

"Getting to know him, are you?"

"Getting to know what he wants me to know.
There's something about this screed that puzzles me.
It might even be honesty."

"Honesty? Bielby?"

"He certainly doesn't overplay the heroics."

"Except by underplaying them. I could take you to
men who would tell you that Bielby couldn't be
honest with himself."

"Who can? I'm beginning to like the chap."

"So did I—in a way. He was a pompous bugger.
And yet—"

"And yet—"

• 5 •

It's the far Cuillins, and they're calling me away—
The lurking hulk of purple islands, cowering in the mist; grey crofters' cabins, that sprawl about the glen; where the dawn comes up like peanuts, outa Glasgae, 'cross the Clyde—I can look at scenery with the rest. I still sometimes go to the Lakes when the autumn is in the bracken. You could get me to Snowdonia most days of the week. But I steer clear of the Hebrides.

I took a job with an easy-going line that was flying WDX Walruses up and down the Western Isles; the board of directors were men I'd flown with. I thought this was the freedom of the skies, where no one was going to point anything more lethal than holiday-makers' binoculars at me.

I saw little but cloud: alto-cumulus cotton-wool, relieved by the odd wad of cirrus kapok. And dizziness in the open spaces . . . Sometimes I did not think I would have the guts to pull the stick. Sometimes I did not think I'd face another touchdown till the fuel ran out. Sometimes I'd be weather-bound for a week in places whose lyrical names were no consolation: Ardlussa and the Sound of Islay. I hadn't

even the comfort of moonshine whisky. I kept a vow
of abstention for twelve months from my day of
demobilization. If I'd carried on as I had been doing,
it would have meant early cirrhosis.

There were days when I was gripping the controls
like the arms of a dentist's chair. So I jacked it in. And
on my journey south, it was on impulse that I got off
the train at Preston. I told myself, since something
inside me seemed to need an excuse, that it was
because I could not stand either my own company or
the drumming of the wheels for another half-hour. It
was an off-chance that the push-and-pull for the Filton
loop was waiting in its bay.

I got off at Filton. I booked in at the Bull, in which
I had never before set foot in my life. And, after a
dreary dinner, I walked out towards the Playground.

Not much had changed in the High Street. There
were shops that were new to me, but not many. Harry
Lester's fish shop had been taken over, modernized
and extended. Noddy's had gone. There was a naked
look about the edge of the slag, because the railings
had disappeared. I looked back towards Elgin Row
and caught sight of my nan, moving about in the
scullery behind an uncurtained window. Nothing
could have brought me to call and make myself
known to her. She was old now, stooping, her bald
patch extended and shining, and she was pulling
herself arthritically about the room, resting heavily
against the corner of the copper boiler. Her skin
showed up unnaturally yellow under the flame of a
poor broken gasmantle.

A few months previously, before the final para-
phernalia of discharge, I had been back to see my

mam. But I didn't stay long. She had grown up. She had grown up in and with the war. She had even done war work: testing French letters at the end of an air nozzle. It was the first time I had ever seen her look as if she belonged to the year in which she was living: a twin-set, and hair permed in the fashion set by the women's utility periodicals. She had taken to smoking—Player's Weights—and even had one lit over the washing-up bowl. She had put on a bit of weight without actually running to fat. Perhaps that was why she had a more contented look than I had ever associated with her. We had corresponded at longish intervals during the war, and there was no breach between us now. The way to keep it like that was for me not to stay long.

But with my nan I could not even have tried. I turned my back on Elgin Row and walked towards the top of Swallow Street. And I saw that a bomb had accounted for numbers 27 to 41. Another house or two had had to be evacuated on either side of the rubble patch on which they had stood. Even the most optimistic of architects would hardly have expected a terrace of Swallow Street, divided, still to stand. I tried to remember who had lived in each of the hovels that had disappeared, but my memory served me badly. I stepped over the threshold of all that was left of 45, because I knew for a certainty that Billy Turner had lived there.

Even the door had gone—used, without doubt, for firewood by good housekeeping neighbours. I went inside—there was enough light from a street lamp for me to see my way, but not enough to bring out any colour—if there was any left: if there had ever been any. Triangular slashes parted the damp and sagging wallpaper. I smelled rotting plaster and the mushroom sweetness of decaying timbers.

Further up the street there were houses still occupied. Radios, muffled and tinny in chimney corners, sounded a variety show.

Then, somewhere at the bottom of the street, I heard frantic feet scampering. I looked and saw a skinny youth, falling over his feet as he ran, clasping one arm with the other. And I saw a black saloon car brake unevenly on the crossroads at the bottom. It reversed into an alley and thrust its nose into Swallow Street: exactly as I had once decoyed old Brewster, I picked up a half-brick and threw it into the furthest corner of a bomb-site, and was rewarded by a minor avalanche. At the same time, I caught the boy in my arms and drew him through the doorway of the wrecked and empty 45.

"What's on, lad?"

"Bloody coppers!"

The car crept up and parked outside the house. Two men in uniform got out and picked their way towards my diversion. I pulled the boy into the deepest patch of shadow. The lower part of his arm was warm and sticky. I dug my thumb into an artery and he winced with pain, tried instinctively to get away from me. To be of any use to him, I had to fight him.

"Plate-glass window, was it? Next time, wrap your hand in a bit of old sacking."

I had no wish to teach him his trade, but I had to get his confidence by some means or other.

"I'm going to make a tourniquet. You haven't cut

an artery, or you wouldn't be arguing with me. But you've run it pretty close. Where do you live, lad?"

"What's that to you?"

"I need to get you there—if the law doesn't get you first."

"Sod that for a lark."

"You want to die out here, do you? Sod that for a lark, too. Address?"

"Elgin Row. Number twelve."

"Maggie Leyland's."

"She's my sister," he said, as if the fact disgusted him. "Listen, mister. I don't want the old woman to find out."

"She might not enjoy your funeral very much, either."

We heard the police clambering about the rubble, then eventually return and start up their car. They must have assumed that the boy had made his way through the ruins into the next street.

"Your Mum and Dad both in?" I asked.

"My Dad's dead."

Sullen. He was a complex of resentment. He didn't mean to tell me more without prompting. I waited. I think he was aware of my rising temper.

"The old woman's in bed. She's been ill for years."

I took him unerringly to the right house. Maggie was sitting at the kitchen table, darning what was virtually a new shoulder for one of his vests. It was an Elgin Row kitchen, an Elgin Row table, scrubbed white, so that the grain of the deal was worn to a relief of primeval channels and valleys. She looked briefly at his arm, without paying close attention to me, started running water into a bowl in the sink.

"You're going to need the strongest disinfectant you can lay your hands on," I said.

I would have recognized her in any setting. She had aged more than I had. But she had the same vaulted forehead, the same curved nose, now more firmly set than the last time I had seen it. She had the same pair of patient eyes—though they were angry with her brother. She was not dressed to receive a visitor. Her hair was parted, but that was all the attention it had had that day, and it had a dog's-leg parting that degenerated into mousey fluffiness under a tortoiseshell clip.

"I'll get him to the doctor in the morning," she said.

"You'd better. I hope he knows how to be discreet. Is it still Dr. Andrews?"

"Heavens, no. He died years ago."

Her brother was regaining his composure.

"Any grub in the house?"

"Something fortifying, I'd suggest. Hot soup, if your sister can manage it."

"Hot soup!" Contemptuous. "Who the hell are you, anyway?"

"Someone you should be glad you ran into," Maggie said. "And keep your voice down, Cliff. There's no need to wake Mum."

There was something in her voice that brought back all I had forgotten. It was not simply her Playground vowels. In my log-rolling years, I'd done my best to eradicate mine; but my voice had never been like Maggie's. Even with such jealous boundaries as those of the Town Moor, there were degrees and differences. Maggie was scrupulous about her final consonants. There was a musical burr about her R's. It brought back the relative gentility of the Leylands. I was lulled. I remember thinking that I could have sat back and listened to her forever. She turned to me.

"Can I get you anything?"

"A cup of Filton tea would go down a treat—when you're through with everything else."

Cliff left half his soup; it was a gesture—he needed to make one. He went upstairs, making more noise than he need have done. Seconds later a feeble voice called down. Maggie excused herself.

Alone, I looked more closely round the room. There was a photograph of the wedding: the dove-grey costumes. There was my nan, looking strangely younger than my memory of her. There was my mam, unbelievably young and drab, her mouth down at the corners. Even old Top-Notch had somehow got himself into the picture. And the picture had been taken only an hour or so before Brewster and the detective had knocked on our door.

On the arm of a chair was the week's *Filton Examiner*. I flicked over its pages. Among the Appointments Vacant was a framed panel, standing out nobly, as befitted a key position on the paper's own staff. They wanted a sub-editor: realistic prospects for an ambitious man.

Maggie, red in the face, came downstairs with a bedpan, over which she had thrown a huckaback towel. She carried it through the scullery to the lavatory in the yard. The smell was unnatural and putrescent.

"I'm sorry about that," she said.

"I'm only sorry your mother's ill."

"She is—very ill. I must go up again and bed her down. Then I'll make the tea and we can talk. That is, if—"

"My time's my own," I said.

She was upstairs a long time. When she came down again, she had changed into an immaculate grey pleated skirt and a ribbed, pale blue home-knitted jumper that fitted her tightly. She had tidied her hair, dabbed a pinkness of powder on her cheeks and reddened her lips.

"Transformation!" I said, and she smiled with a mixture of pleasure and embarrassment. Compliments were not common currency on the Town Moor. I looked at her directly, not sparing her the knowledge that I was appraising her. She blushed again—then smiled.

"How old is Cliff?"

"Fourteen."

"And how long since his father died?"

"More than ten years ago. He was three."

"He'll need an anti-tetanus jab."

"It ought to be done tonight."

"He'll be under arrest in half an hour if you take him to Casualty while they're still looking. Get him to the surgery first thing in the morning."

"You know a lot about these things, don't you?"

"About breaking the law, you mean?"

"No. I mean the way you looked after Cliff."

"I did once dig a bullet out of a flight-sergeant's heel with a pen-knife."

She brewed the tea—stiff, strong, Elgin Row stuff.

"Do you mind if we talk about Cliff?"

"Talk on," I said, rejoicing in the music.

"I've tried to appeal to him with all kinds of thing."

"Such as?"

"Taking a pride in his school work. Gymnastics at the Boys' Club. Joining the ATC. Thinking about what job he wants to do."

"Kids' stuff!"

"I don't think it's kids' stuff at all. Other boys do these things."

"You're trying to entice him with the very things he's rebelling against."

"Why should he want to rebel?"

"Don't you, ever?"

"Why should I? It's obvious what my job is."

I looked at my watch. It was after midnight. There had been a notice at the Bull which said they had no night porter. I should have asked for a key.

"You can stay here." Maggie was eager that I should. "I can easily manage you a bed."

"You have enough on your hands as it is."

"You can have my bed. I'll sleep down here."

And then she attempted a touch of roguishness.

"After all, you gave up your bed for me, once."

A mule-kick. I had been certain that I was unrecognizable in Filton. I was a head taller than when I had left. I had filled out. My face had changed shape. My hair was anybody's colour. There was nothing about me to suggest the spidery lout who had left here in the thirties.

"I know you're Sid Wheeler."

"Roger Bielby, Maggie. I don't want Sid Wheeler ever to catch up with me."

"He won't. Nobody would know you. And don't be ashamed of those days—Roger. I know people used to think you were a bit of a handful. But we understood—some of us. And you did rise above it—as I can't see Cliff ever doing. You even won a decoration, didn't you? Your nan used to tell us your news. She was so proud of you."

"Pity! I didn't do it for her pleasure."

And Maggie looked momentarily shocked. That wasn't an attitude that the Leylands had towards anyone.

"Are you likely to be here long, Roger?"

"I've come for an interview. For a job on the *Examiner*."

I spoke as if the project had been on my mind for weeks.

"Will you try to help me with Cliff?"

Nothing had been spent on Maggie's room since she had grown up in it. The pictures on the walls—sports girls of the nineteen-twenties, cuddling spaniels and tennis rackets—were giveaways from the women's magazines, home-framed in passepartout. Every item of furniture had once been someone's pride or sacrifice. Now nothing matched, and everything had deteriorated from the damp that was the running enemy along the Row. She had a few books: *The Story of San Michele* and one or two wartime Penguins. Otherwise the only personal touch was a wisp of hair from a comb, loose in a lidless glass powder bowl.

I slept well in Maggie's bed. We had talked late. But I woke sharply, of habit, at seven. I stood and looked out over the Playground, this angle new to me, since Maggie lived higher up the Row than we had. I was surprised by the smallness of the Town Moor world in the monochrome of morning. My memory had preserved the grass as longer and greener, less flatly trampled into the sifted shale. The yards down the Row were a huddle of arbitrary angles: broken hinges, hutches, kennels and downpipes.

I went down in my vest and trousers to wash in the scullery. Maggie was stirring the lumps out of a bland invalid food. She fried me a breakfast that must have made appalling inroads into the rations.

I made no promises about coming back. I, who had run away from Sally Carver, was in no position to make positive dispositions about Maggie Leyland. I watched her as she moved about the room. She had again put on the skirt and jumper of yesterday evening. It must have been a desperate decision; they could be the only presentable clothes she had. We talked pleasantly, but I cannot say that last night's euphoria at the sound of her voice persisted.

Before I left, I had to be taken up to see Maggie's mum. One needed no special knowledge of medicine or life to see how things stood with her. The skin was so tightly stretched across her forehead that I had the illusion of looking through translucency to bone. It was hard to imagine that her body had any resource left on which she still could draw. But her weakness had affected neither her intelligence nor her memory. She called me Sid Wheeler and she knew the rough shape of what had happened to me since I had last been in Filton. And she was glad to see me. Maggie's mum always had been. She had always treated me as if she thought that I was normal.

"And how's your mam?"

"She's very well. She sends her love."

"Give her mine, next time you see her."

"I will, Mrs. Leyland."

Old Jethro Burgess of the *Examiner* liked me. I had
only to satisfy him—and preserve strict political
independence—and I could aspire to be his assistant
editor within two years. He was very proud of the
Examiner's freedom from strings.

I made a number of visits to Elgin Row, usually
under cover of darkness. My relationship with Maggie was a paradox. Half of me tried to rationalize
myself, to argue that she was inappropriate for me,
that all that attracted me was the sublime ease with
which I could make an impression. And yet I was
drawn back to her and back again; it was compulsive.

I seemed, too, to develop a genius for showing up
at Elgin Row at fateful moments. One of my rare
daytime visits coincided with the steaming prepara-
tions for a blanket-bath. A sick-room crisis would be
the moment that I chose to knock. I happened in on
Cliff at bad moments, and brushed with him at his
most truculent. I began to be bored by Maggie's
repetitious tales of his intractability; and yet in another way I welcomed them, for they gave me
leverage with her. What nearly kept me away from
12, Elgin Row for good and all was the apparent
impossibility of getting Maggie to make—or accept—
any arrangement that would allow me to take her off
the Town Moor for an hour or two. She had a
puritanical attachment to the virtues of slavery. She
regarded home-nursing as a twenty-four hours a day
duty. Any defection was a mortal sin—and a mortal

peril for her patient. We had one particular argument about it that developed into anger on both sides. She was adamant about the impossibility of coming out for an hour in the evening with me. I left her in tears, and it was a fortnight before I went to see her again. When I did (I had persuaded myself that I wasn't going to) I found her tearful and amenable at last, albeit uneasy.

There was an old crow in a corner-house on Swallow Street, a certain Martha Garbutt, on call for everything from reading tea-leaves to pragmatic mid-wifery and philosophical laying-out. She was well known as a hater of men, whom she blamed for all the ills that ever afflicted woman. Maggie had her provisionally lined up as a mother-sitter.

Old Jethro loaned me his car for the outing, a black and bashed-up pre-war Humber that was in communal use on *Examiner* business. I drove north-east out of Filton, dipping into gritstone valleys, and we swept up to the moors that rippled with sparse cotton grass and wiry heather.

Maggie was too small-framed for elegance, too naturally prim to be exciting; she could never look exotic. Her hair was simply styled, with a single blue band across it that did all that was necessary to relieve its plainness. There was a natural simplicity about her that charmed me; she was saved from severity by the warmth of her complexion.

Spring had been tardy this year, but it was now well advanced. I pulled up once so that we could stand by a stone wall and look out over the coastal plain. The old gold of sunset slashed the Ribble estuary and eastwards from us the bracken rolled far away into

Yorkshire in an infinity of young greens. A lapwing screamed, wheeling away from us. The curlew's cry brought back something from boyhood to which I could put neither name nor occasion.

And Maggie's conscience gave her no peace. "If only I could lose the feeling that I ought not to be here—"

Presently I pulled up again on a grass verge. We had reached one of those spots of high ground where the land stretched away in overlapping folds in every direction. To our left lay a still-life group of farm roofs; to our right the ruin of a one-time shepherd's hut. She got out of the car and walked a few yards from me, a slight, trim, insignificant yet firm figure, against the immensity of a backcloth that had changed very little since the recession of the Ice Age. And, good God, I ought to have known how to make a physical approach to her! When had I ever been afraid of contact with a girl? Couldn't I draw at least on the training I had had from Sally Carver? Or was I paralysed because I believed that failure now could deprive me of Maggie Leyland for ever?

I climbed out of the car a few seconds after her, and as I set foot on the springy peat soil, the whole hemisphere of Pennine sky began to sway over me. I rocked with that dizziness in space from which I thought I had recovered in the welter of activity of the last few months.

I plunged forward, not knowing where I was setting my feet. Coming up behind Maggie, I put my arm about her shoulder, closing my hand over her wrist. She did not look back at me, and when I looked down sideways into her face, I saw that there were tears welling up into her eyes. And I knew that for her as well as for me it was all too much, the solitude, the unspoiled savagery and the palette of nature's colours. We needed now the other thing that was missing from our lives. We kissed, the bastard and the love-child, in a wilderness both as full and empty as an open ocean.

I had reserved us a table at the Black Sedge, an expensive and fashionable Free House in the Trough of Bowland, a wild tract on the Lancashire-Yorkshire border; fast and noisy torrents over tumbled boulders. There was an enlivening chill in the air as we got out into a car-park bounded by twee and unconvincing little cairns. Of necessity Maggie was a virtual teetotaller, and she was delighted by her first Cinzano. She started to talk as if the conversational needs of years were offered half an hour's relief. She asked me questions, gave me every opportunity that I could crave to talk big. When we were at last called to our table, she gave a little murmur of delight at the decor—stubby red candles flickering against the wainscoting, surmounted by antlers and squares of hunting tartan. We had what they called minestrone; we weren't critical. And when I asked for a roll to crumble about the table-cloth, it was brought for me in a basket lined with red paper napkins. Maggie held up her glass and watched the distorted candle flame flickering in the depths of her Châteauneuf du Pape.

"You've learned a lot about things, haven't you, Roger?"

"If it hadn't been for the war—"

"Apart from that, you went down South—"

"Essex wasn't all that magical."

"I would have thought that anything seemed magical after the Town Moor."

"I wished myself back here more often than I wished myself anywhere else."

I called for the menu again after our main dish and explained to her the difference between a *glace* and a *bombe*. For myself, I asked for a savoury. The waiter looked at me with what I took to be a deep personal satisfaction that riled me beyond toleration.

"I'm sorry, sir. The bread you had with your soup has to count as a full course."

Bread in these austerity years had recently been rationed, and one of the exasperating regulations was what he had just quoted at me. I tore into that waiter. It was not an act that I was putting on to impress Maggie. Far to the contrary, I was reckless of the impression that I was creating. It was an onrush of temper that expended a long accumulation of suspense and frustration. And it was the insolent pleasure on the waiter's face that lit the fuse. The landlord came, urbane and winsomely soft-tongued.

"You see how it is, sir. The Golden Fleece was shopped only last week. How'm I to know that you're not from the *Gestapo* yourself?"

It was fatally the wrong word to use to me. I was carried headlong by the momentum of my fury. But Maggie intervened, with a sweet and unanswerable simplicity.

"He isn't," she said.

They brought me my cheese on toast, though by then I had no stomach for it and could neither chew nor swallow. I apologized to Maggie for the embarrassment that I had caused her—and then I went on to try to justify myself. But she refused to be concerned.

"What does it matter, Roger? Let's forget it: just a little bit of bread."

She picked her way exploratively through the dye-stuffs of her ice and then, sipping coffee in the lounge, floundering in deep-sunken armchairs at impossibly low tables, we reminded each other of recent radio jokes and catch-phrases. It was desultory stuff. Maggie did not want a liqueur; and I went without. She looked at the clock—permanently kept ten minutes fast—and said that she thought it was time we should be going. Martha Garbutt or no Martha Garbutt, she was bound to disturb her mother when she went in, and already she was beginning to be haunted by notions of what disasters might have happened in her absence. We drove back across the moors. The curve of cat's-eyes leaped up under the bonnet, moths swept suicidally into the windscreen; a rabbit's rump bounded for cover, its upturned tail bleached white in the spear of the headlamps.

I stopped in the pitch darkness, approximately where I judged the shepherd's hut to be, and leaned over and kissed her. She was moderately responsive; and I knew that it was not with any intent to repulse me that she pleaded again for us not to be any later. I disciplined myself, knocked the lever into gear.

As soon as we arrived in sight of Elgin Row we could see that something was amiss. There were lights on all over the house, even in the front room.

Cliff was sitting at the kitchen table, his face untypically pale. Martha Garbutt, who had been lumbering up the stairs as we entered, turned and

came down again, a pair of nail scissors in one hand,
face-flannel and towel in the other.

"Aye, well," she said. "It's to be hoped that you've
come home well fortified."

Maggie's Mum had died while I had been thunder-
ing about the bread ration.

It was here that Bielby's manuscript came to an end.
At this point he was taken out of his cell, on his way
to the committal proceedings that he never reached.

Superintendent Bartram seemed compelled not to let
Kenworthy out of his sight and care for too long a
time. He was knocking on the door of the private
office as Kenworthy turned the last page of Bielby's
script.

"Well, Man of the Yard—now you know—"

"No. Now I don't know. I know less than ever!"

Bartram blew out his cheeks, heightening the effect
of his clown's face.

"Oh, come, Kenworthy. Ask yourself what mo-
tives he had for writing this."

"To pass his time. To stand back and take a long
cool look at things. Perhaps to convince us—"

"And to get into paperback before his trial was
forgotten. To have a little pile of royalties waiting for
him when he'd done his bird."

"Perhaps to try to convince himself as well as us,"
Kenworthy said. "I kept finding little anomalies. Like
signing a twelve-month pledge on one page and
knocking back the vermouth and Châteauneuf on the
next."

"Typical. Bielby only had to say a thing to believe

it. Trouble was, he took a lot of others along with him."

"And yet I kept ploughing my nose into what looked embarrassingly like a furrow of sincerity."

"Exactly what I mean. I told you a little while ago that I liked the man. I did. And yet he was a shite-hawk. He was a journalist, Kenworthy. He could have been a top-liner, if he'd stuck to it. He had mass hysteria at his fingertips. Wouldn't you have enjoyed this pulp romance of his a little more if there'd been a hint of remorse in it somewhere?"

Kenworthy picked up the manuscript as if he were going to remind himself of some point, then apparently changed his mind and laid it down again.

"You'd hardly expect him to write a confession, would you?" Bartram said.

"He didn't finish his story. Not by a long way. Everything a man writes is a confession in one way or another. If only the reader can see it."

"You're surely not questioning the obvious about Maggie Bielby's murder?"

"When things look obvious, I often amuse myself by digging about in opposites," Kenworthy said. "I suppose it's one way of relieving the boredom."

He suddenly stirred himself, as if his own attitudinizing was boring him too. He spoke more briskly.

"Fill me in on a thing or two. Evidently Bielby became the bright star of the *Filton Examiner*—"

"He did that. Old Jethro Burgess was a giant in his way. One of the last of the great eccentrics, but he knew where he was pointed. I was surprised that he let Bielby take him in in the way that he did. I suppose he'd grown tired. Bielby was assistant editor in no time."

"In spite of the ban Burgess put on political participation?"

"Bielby was too crafty to be hog-tied. Politically, he called himself independent. And the way the parties are finely balanced here, that gave him a lot of power, bargaining behind the scenes. And tying it all up with what he was pushing in the *Examiner*."

"And what colour was that?"

"Popular reaction: playing to the Filton Dress Circle. Those were the days of the Attlee government: welfare state, nationalization and bureaucracy. There was plenty for Bielby to knock. Take education: he was dead against wastage of public money, especially on adult education. Why should evening classes be provided with golfballs and oil paints out of the public purse? Bielby pushed it to extremes. He ran a campaign against the Evening Institute that went on for months. It went down big. He knew how to choose a ripe issue. Take St. Luke's Playground, that patch of crappy slag—"

Bartram heard feet in the corridor and called to a passing constable to bring him a packet of cigarettes from the canteen.

"Take St. Luke's Playground. There was a scheme just after the war to knock all that property down and house the occupants up on the new Coldsprings Estate. Bielby opposed it. He manipulated the opposition, had public meetings called, made it an issue in the *Examiner*, piped out a lot of sentimental tripe about organic communities. They weren't going to be allowed to keep domestic pets up on Coldsprings: he made a lot of that. The result was that it cost the ratepayer a packet in the end. Mawdesley, the landowner, offered the whole site to the Borough for thirty thousand, back in 1947, when he wanted to get the slums off his hands before he had to do something with them. The rehousing scheme went down by a couple of votes and the Council declined. The area was bought up by a faceless syndicate who kept it on ice till the time was ripe. And when the Town Moor Shopping Centre was conceived—this time with Bielby's full support—they had to give two hundred thousand for it. Bielby had a lot to answer for."

"And his progress on the *Examiner* was rapid?"

"Assistant editor in eighteen months, and to all intents and purposes he was sitting in the editor's chair before Burgess retired. When we arrested him, he was still nominally caretaker-editor while the executors were sorting out the Burgess estate. But for several years he'd had a professional deputy to do all the drudgery. It was intrigue and influence that filled Bielby's life."

"And he was never in danger of the ghost of Sid Wheeler?"

Bartram pulled the sort of face that would have suited the act of hawking into sawdust.

"Sid Wheeler amounted to nothing. The name wouldn't have been remembered in Filton outside those three grotty streets. If Bielby ever thought that his brand of pre-war delinquency amounted to anything, then he was suffering from delusions of grandeur. His identity never would have come out, if it hadn't been for the old woman. And by then, Bielby was a big enough cheese to wear it—alongside his

DFC. Ten minutes' embarrassment, and he was capitalizing on it. Local boy wins through. 'I pulled myself up by my shoe-tags; why can't you lot?' "

"If it hadn't been for the old woman?" Kenworthy prompted.

"His *nan*. He'd never been to see her: so much for the organic family. But when the Town Moor Development finally did get off the ground, she was the one who refused to be evicted. The bulldozer was up to the party walls on either side. The telly Outside Broadcasts van was parked in what was left of Elgin Row. And Bielby, because he was then Chairman of Housing, had to be the one to go in and talk her out. And, big noise though he always was in public, he was always a bellyful of worms on the final approach. Before he ever made an after-dinner speech, his legs were all twisted up under the table. But give him his due, he could whip himself up into doing what was needed."

Bartram's cigarettes arrived. He offered one to Kenworthy, but Kenworthy preferred his pipe.

"The old girl was well into her eighties, and losing her faculties: but she knew what was going on. You never know where you stand with these so-called seniles. They had to manhandle her out of the house, Bielby putting his arm round her shoulders for the sake of the TV cameras. And she's standing there, her bald patch flaming red, just as Bielby put it down on paper, her nose and chin practically meeting; and she's shouting at the top of her voice, 'We all know whose bastard you are, Sid Wheeler!' And a lot of other things that didn't mean a thing to anyone. But there were bystanders on the Town Moor who didn't need telling a second time. Bielby had to face it out and dig into his ingenuity. The way he handled it, interviewed on *Tonight* and all that, he turned it more to his good than his harm. Born to survive—"

"Except in the police station yard—"

Kenworthy hunted in every pocket for his smoker's knife, which was lying on the desk in front of him.

"And who's been backing Bielby all these years? He was a front man, if ever there was one. Who was his paymaster? You seem to think it didn't all come from Burgess. You mentioned just now a faceless syndicate. Who was pulling Bielby's strings?"

"This," Bartram said, "is where a long standing resident like myself is not sorry they've brought in an outsider to agitate the pooh."

"But you do know, Superintendent, don't you? You *must* know—"

"A few years ago I'd have said I did: Mawdesley. But Mawdesley went to gaol—and Bielby's name was never breathed; not even behind the scenes. And Bielby went on spending more than Burgess could possibly have been paying him."

"The same Mawdesley that you mentioned just now? Who tried to sell the Town Moor? And had Bielby up against him?"

"It was an odd thing—yet perhaps not so odd. They first met in opposition—and ended up admiring each other. There's no doubt that Mawdesley was Bielby's mentor in Filton's spheres of influence."

"And this estimable gentleman is now out and about again?"

"He got five years, was a good boy and did three

years four months. He came out about this time last
year."

"And weren't there any papers on Bielby that went
to the DPP, the way these things do, only to be
chucked out for want of key evidence?"

"Bielby was as clean as a whistle."

"In fact, it was his innocence that had always
earned him his keep?"

"Innocence?"

Bartram's eyes bulged with clownish gravity.

"Innocence. That's it. A lot of people in Filton
thought Bielby was a nice chap. I even went that way
myself, once or twice. But you do things your own
way, Kenworthy. I don't want to pre-empt you. Just
bear in mind that I might know the answers to some
questions that you haven't thought of asking yet."

• 6 •

KENWORTHY HAD A small London team with him whom he did not know well: there had been some rapid promotion in the last few years for those who had kept their noses clean enough to stay in the force. Inspector Heald was a cool, unexpansive, unselfrevealing man who had the reputation of a devoted technician. His great joy was to get all his known and supposed factors into charts where he could keep his eye on them, now and then firmly planting a cross that eliminated two columns at once. There were two sergeants, Cooper and Widgeon. And it was the youth of today's sergeants, Kenworthy reflected, that reminded him how near was his own retirement. He knew next to nothing about them, except that they had argued interminably about politics throughout the journey, neither paying an atom of attention to what the other said. Cooper was a romantic progressive; Widgeon an elitist. Finally, there was Patsy Morley, who was supposed to take clerical weight off them all; especially if something blew up that had better not be handled by Bartram's clerks.

He set Inspector Heald, with Cooper as long-stop,

on a fundamental review of the killing of Bielby's wife, treating it as nearly as imagination would allow as an initial investigation. He sent Widgeon up on to the roof from which Bielby had been shot. WPC Morley typed Heald's tabulated charts as he drafted them. Kenworthy rapidly established a reputation for mere ruminative idleness.

There were too many, either for comfort or effectiveness, in the party that accompanied his first visit to Bielby's home. In addition to himself, Heald and Cooper, there had to be Gibson, the Filton Inspector who had led all the ground-work in the first instance. In the absence of contra-indications, he had a prescriptive right to be present, and he too brought his sergeant, a mercifully silent man called Underwood. Consequently there were five of them moving from room to room as Kenworthy was taken on his tour of inspection.

Sandringham Avenue lay in the inner heart of Filton's most exclusive speculative estate, reached after the two right-angles of Chatsworth and Balmoral. *Notre Repos* had been built in the late 1950s, with a strong nostalgia for the Metroland of the 30s: double-fronted commuter's open timber, with a crunching drive of pea-gravel. An elderly man in a grey pullover was mowing the lawn, which had outgrown itself into seeded grasses nearly two feet high. He switched off his two-stroke engine and came over briskly the moment they pushed open the gate.

"I hope I'm not doing the wrong thing. They'll need it looking trim for the estate agent, and if it grows much more, it'll be a hay-field. I did mention it to Mr. Bielby Junior, and he said carry on."

"Very neighbourly of you, I'm sure," the Filton Inspector said.

"If I can be of any assistance at all to you gentlemen—"

"Thank you. I'm sure we can manage."

Lorimer made himself scarce with polite alacrity. It was he who had telephoned about the shot, he who had rushed in and found Biebly with the warm pistol in his hand. He had also been informative, down to the last meticulous detail, about the recent mobile evening habits both of Bielby and his wife's visitors. The not-so-long-retired company secretary of a paint factory on the outskirts of Wigan, he was finding his present life in Sandringham Avenue none too demanding.

Inspector Gibson had a tagged key and stooped to pick up correspondence from the hall floor: Reader's Digest circulars, a telephone account, a monthly book club choice. The house smelled of dust—dust on the handset of the prestige model telephone, dust on the handrail of the open-tread staircase. The furnishings were near-contemporary. Bielby, in his initial statement, as in subsequent amendments, had insisted that when he had come in that night, he had found things in some disarray, but there was no sign of that now. Everything was clinically tidy, fitted carpets immaculate. Art was Tretchikoff, reproduction Lowry and Camarguish horses. There were one or two expensive reproduction pieces—a corner cupboard (for drinks) and a Jacobean footstool—but no sense of unity or co-ordination. There was not a single stick of furniture that looked as if it was of Town Moor provenance, the only taproot to Elgin Row being the

photograph of Mrs. Leyland's wedding, which hung
in a single-bedded and apparently rarely used spare
room.

It was a house drained shockingly and suddenly of
its life, of its soul. And yet had it ever had either? It
was a house in which expense had not been spared—
in which expense and the evidence were the substitute
for comfort. Bielby's home belonged to this year, not
last, the criteria stemming from the Sunday supple-
ments: etched silver plaques of vintage London om-
nibuses; a reproduction carriage clock in patent polished brass. Dusty and deserted, but nothing out of
place; no sign that anything here had ever been *used*.
Only in the kitchen was there evidence of life's blood.
A ribbed gleam of stainless steel; and a range of
copper-bottomed saucepans that could surely not have
been out of their polystyrene packing for more than a
week or two. But there were shopping notes, memos
from Maggie to Maggie, clipped to the wall, a pile of
women's magazines, a knocked-about transistor radio
untidily askew on a plain wood table.

Kenworthy casually picked up one or two of the
bits and pieces of Maggie's existence, moved over
and ran his fingertips through a dent in the glossy
paintwork of the kitchen door, let his eyes stray in the
direction of one of the chairs.

Up in the murder bedroom, Kenworthy opened the
window. There was a curious fustiness, complicated
by the smell of the sort of spray that undertakers use,
originally cloying, now stale. The bed had remained
stripped down to its mattress, from which an irregular
polygon of the covering had been cut away.

He held out his hand for the clip-board which his

Inspector Heald was carrying, the top sheet a schedule of events on the last night when Roger Bielby had visited his mistress:

1900 hours	John Henry Fielding left home for Crown and Cushion Club. (Source, J. H. Fielding, Lucette Fielding.)
1950 approx	J. H. Fielding arrived Crown and Cushion. (Source JHF; club members generally.)
2010 approx	Bielby left Crown and Cushion, having drunk more than was usual for him at that time of evening. (Source, club steward and members.)
2020 approx	Bielby arrived at Fielding's home. (Source, Bielby; Lucette Fielding.)
2045	Car arrived on Bielby's drive, as had happened on about four evenings of previous week at about this time. (Source, Lorimer.)
2145	Car drove away from *Notre Repos*. On previous occasions, it had not left until about 2330. (Source, Lorimer.)
2200 approx	Phone call received by Bielby at Fielding's house. (See extended statement by L. Fielding.) Bielby had arrived nearer drunk than Mrs. Fielding had ever seen him before, then had drunk three-quarters of bottle of Sauternes with the light

supper she had given him; stiff
brandy with coffee afterwards.
Phone call had taken both parties
by surprise, as they had thought
secrecy of these visits inviolate.
(Note by Insp. Gibson: known to
most of residents in road.) Bielby
enraged by nature of phone call,
which remains unknown to Mrs.
Fielding. Bielby obstinately refused to give any information under questioning. (Source, L.
Fielding.)

2225
approx

Bielby left Mrs. Fielding in
drunken fury. Said, "Sorry, I shall
have to go home, the bitch."
(Source, L. Fielding.)

2230-2234
approx

Bielby arrived home. States that he
found front door open and some
disarrangement of downstairs furniture. (Source, Bielby.)

2233
(timing
exact)

Shot heard in *Notre Repos*.
(Source, Lorimer; other neighbours confirm, but not so precise
re timing.)

2234
(timing
exact)

Lorimer dialled 999. (Source,
Lorimer; HQ log.)

2236

Lorimer entered *Notre Repos* to
investigate. (Source, Lorimer and
Mrs. Lorimer.) Found Bielby
standing by wife's body by bed

	with automatic pistol in hand. (Source, Lorimer.)
2238	Arrival of squad car, PC's Forbes and Rossiter. (Radio log.)
2245	Arrival of Insp. Gibson (log). Interviews with Bielby who was barely articulate and Lorimer (statements on file).
2300	Bielby taken to station for questioning. More articulate, to some extent sobered by events. Initial statement taken from hesitant dictation. Bielby had difficulty in remaining awake. Revived with strong black coffee. (Log and file.)
0730	Bielby visited in cell with breakfast. Shaky, demanded release, and asked for short alcoholic drink. Requests refused. Allowed to ring solicitor— Jeremy Hibbert—whom he had declined to contact overnight. Hibbert still in bed. (File; station incident book.)
0800	Hibbert arrived at station and advised Bielby to say nothing further whatever. Also requested that Bielby be either released or charged. (File: station incident book.)
0915	Insp. Gibson interviewed Lucette Fielding at her home. She badly frightened; prevaricated. (File)
0947	L. Fielding made definitive statement. (File)

1020   Bielby charged. (File and incident book.)

1430   Bielby remanded in custody at specially convened magistrates' court.

Kenworthy handed the clip-board back to Heald.

"Too many people in here," he said. "I want a word with Inspector Gibson. The rest of you scarper."

Gibson was a responsible-looking and unhurried man in his middle thirties.

"Let's go downstairs," Kenworthy said. "This room depresses me."

A minute later they were both sitting in the Bielbys' armchairs, their heels on the Bielbys' carpet, their tobacco ash in the Bielbys' ashtrays.

"I know your log by heart," Kenworthy said, "but there's something it doesn't tell me."

The inspector's eyebrows were raised in expectation of fault-finding. He looked like a man who would defend himself energetically.

"You had a busy night—but I don't know at what stages you consulted your superiors."

"We've kept the abstracts from the file as simple as we could for your sake, Chief Superintendent."

"I'm not getting at you, Inspector. It's just that I'm intrigued. You were in this house eleven minutes after your switchboard took the emergency call. That's pretty good going. And Forbes and Rossiter did even better. They made it in four minutes."

"They were cruising less than a mile away. I'd have made it quicker, but the station was short of transport. I had to come on foot."

"Then you must have been running. Your first murder?"

"Of any consequence. The others have all been desperate-domestic."

"Desperate-domestic? You don't think this was, then?"

"Well, of course, in a sense—"

Again, he suspected that he was about to be got at. And he was not mollified by Kenworthy's smile.

"What you really mean, was that this has the hallmark of Bielby."

"Bielby was a bigwig, certainly."

"So at what stage did you feel that you had better let it be known higher up what sort of dynamite you were handling?"

"I rang Superintendent Bartram at home as soon as I had Bielby at the station."

"At about eleven o'clock, in fact?"

"That's right. And he was over in about ten minutes. And by then I had alerted County, for information of Detective Superintendent Hallam. That's drill."

"Quite. So did Superintendent Bartram look in on your interrogation of Bielby?"

"He looked in and just told me to carry on. He was disgusted at the state Bielby was in. And as soon as he heard the circumstances and saw how things stood, he just said it was a case of waiting for Bielby to incriminate himself."

"And your Detective-Superintendent?"

"It took him longer to get here. He'd been at a dinner in Lancaster. It was half past two before he showed up."

"Whilst you were still working on Bielby?"

"Trying to. I was hoping to trap him while he was still fuddled. When Superintendent Hallam came, we were just trying to get some more black coffee into him, and he had vomited over himself."

"Did you clean him up?"

"Not at once. I thought that a little discomfort—"

"And Superintendent Hallam did not tell you to desist?"

"No, sir. Should he have done?"

"Well, I wouldn't, in his place. I'd have either left you to it or joined in the fun."

"Well, that's what he did, Mr. Kenworthy, both. He had a go at him in the same vein that I was using, then he told me to keep up the good work."

"A wise Superintendent."

"Then he went off and talked to Superintendent Bartram. He looked in on us again at half past three, and said he was going home to bed. There was no need for me to ring him before eight-thirty, and he'd be along here soon after that, anyway. I actually contacted him again as soon as I had the statement from Mrs. Fielding."

"Yes, I meant to ask you that. What put you on to her?"

"It was common talk in the town, sir. Bielby was the most bitter anti-Catholic in the Borough; and here he was laying the most influential of the bunch. About the only Filtonians who didn't know what was going on were Fielding himself—and, I'd have guessed, Maggie Bielby."

"I liked your timing, Inspector. Nine-fifteen: I

presume you didn't want to call on her until her husband had gone to work."

"Correct. And as soon as Superintendent Hallam had heard about the phone call that Bielby had taken at her home, he said, 'That's enough to be going on with. Charge him.' "

"Pity."

"Why on earth?"

"Because if you hadn't charged him, he'd probably still be alive."

"But, sir—"

"I've always found it a valuable exercise, Inspector, before I've ever charged anyone, to take a quiet few minutes in a corner and picture myself as the lawyer who has to try to get him off. What would my case be?"

"You're surely not suggesting that Bielby was innocent?"

"I'm not suggesting that at all—because I simply don't know yet. What I am suggesting is that if I'd been his defending counsel, I'd have felt optimistic. This question of furniture in disarray when Bielby entered the house: he insisted on it?"

"Very strongly—in a drink-fuddled way."

"Did you see any evidence of it?"

"None at all. The house was as tidy as it is now."

"And Lorimer's impression? After all, he was in here before you?"

"He'll tell you what I've told you. There was no disorder, and Bielby was in an alcoholic fog."

"Will you just sit there, Inspector, and try not to feel self-conscious—or make me feel self-conscious—while I do something daft?"

Gibson looked at him with a sort of patient credulity. Kenworthy went out of the house by the front door and there followed a minute or two of silence before his feet made themselves heard, crunching unevenly in the gravel of the drive. He put one foot down so noisily just inside the hall that Gibson looked up anxiously. But Kenworthy was only play-acting. He came lurching into the lounge, aping a drunken man, picked up a chair, put it down again, stooped as if picking something up, pushed a nonexistent book back into a shelf, bent down again, blowing out through puffed cheeks, pretended to pick up something else. Then he straightened himself, looked at Gibson as if he saw through him and walked with exaggerated care towards the kitchen, like a man trying to prove that he can toe a chalk-line. When he reached the door, he grasped its edge and appeared to be wrestling with it, eventually pushing himself round it as if it were jammed against something. Gibson heard him apparently kick a couple of kitchen chairs. Then he switched on the transistor radio for a brief instant, came back into the lounge, still acting the stage drunk, still behaving as if his colleague were not there. When he reached the door that led into the hall, he suddenly reverted to his brisk yet quiet self. His body seemed to relax and he even appeared to have grown an inch taller.

"Fine," he said. "Forgive that charade, Inspector. Now I'm going to do it all again, and this time I want you to time me. From when I stamp my foot to when I say *Up!*"

He went through the sequence again with the precision of an actor who does not alter a detail of his performance over a year's run. He moved chairs, switched the radio off and on, put back imaginary books, fought the kitchen door. Then, as he came back into the room, he shouted *Up!* again.

"Thirty-six seconds," said the Inspector, who had been sitting all this time with his eyes almost pathologically fixed on his wrist-watch. Kenworthy disappeared up the stairs. When he came back he said, "Now I want the timing of something else."

Upstairs again. *Now!* This time he leaped down the stairs with the silence and agility of a cat, took one stride out of the front door. *Up!*

"Four seconds."

"You might think that that was just an academic exercise, Inspector. Well, maybe it was, but it's worth a moment's consideration. Because if by any chance it was someone other than Bielby who killed his wife, then that someone was actually in the house when he came in. So it would be to our advantage to know how he might have tackled it."

Gibson looked as if it would need a lot to convince him.

"Through the landing window, you can see when anyone passes under the street-lamp outside. That is the moment when he chooses to pull the trigger, as is consonant with Bielby's own account of events. He hears a shot, but he can't tell whether it's upstairs or downstairs. After all, remember how difficult your colleagues on the spot found it to position the shot that got Bielby himself in your yard. He hears this shot and he comes staggering up through the gravel. He finds the front door open and all the lights in the house on. He told you that himself, but you either saw no

significance in it or did not believe him. And maybe
I don't blame you for that; but it could have been true.
He comes into the house, befuddled, doesn't know
what the hell's happened. And he's an almost neurotically tidy man. That's a common syndrome with the
big bully who's basically scared of his own inade-
quacy. Didn't he win something for foot-drill at his
RAF Training Wing? Didn't he once put a flight
sergeant on a charge for poor turn-out? A man like
that doesn't pass a chair that's on its side; especially if
it's in his way. He picks it up. He switches off a radio
that's playing to an empty room. He puts back books
that are lying on the floor where he might tread on
them. You see, I don't think there was a lot of
disruption: just enough to offend his sense of order.
And to get in his way. He sees that the kitchen light's
on, and the door ajar. And that's where he expects his
wife to be. She's a simple, quiet, domesticated soul.
You can bet your life that she spends more time in the
kitchen than anywhere else—just as she always did in
Elgin Row. Damn it, it's the only room in the house
that shows any sign of being lived in. And he'd hardly
expect her to be in bed, would he, since she's just
telephoned him on what seems to have been an
emergency matter? So that's where Bielby makes his
bee-line. And then he finds that the door's stuck
against something—an arrangement of chairs—so he
can't quite squeeze his bulk through. He wriggles in,
moves the chairs, doesn't find Maggie there. Switches
off the radio."

"How do you know the radio was playing?"

"It would be, wouldn't it," Kenworthy said.
"Don't you think? And only now does he go upstairs,

behaving exactly as the murderer has planned. The sheet's across Maggie's face, and the pistol lying across it, so he has to pick it up to uncover her. Perhaps he touched her cheek, feels her pulse, listens for breath—still holding the pistol. He was still holding it a minute or two later, when Lorimer found him."

"All this is highly hypothetical," Gibson said.

"But within the bounds of possibility. Or do you not think so?"

"It would need a lot of thinking through. Would a man, just having heard a shot, stop to rearrange furniture?"

"He might, if his track had been signposted to the kitchen door, and the stuff was lying in his path."

Then Kenworthy suddenly dropped his intensity, and appeared to laugh at himself.

"You must make allowances for me, Inspector. Most of my working life I've had a good sergeant to protect me from my imagination. That's how I've got into the habit of indulging it. So please shoot me down in flames if you think I'm making a bloody idiot of myself."

"Have you spotted something that we've missed?" Gibson asked.

"Come with me."

Kenworthy took him into the kitchen and showed him an indentation on the inside of the door. There was a depression in the woodwork, as might have been made by firm pressure. He now went to the nearest kitchen chair and pointed out that its back had been slightly scratched. A small triangle of cream paint was adhering to it.

"I happened to notice that earlier this morning. It's recent. And it put the rest of the sequence into my mind."

"A feasible reconstruction—but slenderly based, I'd say. How much can we be positive about?"

"That there could be an alternative to Bielby as murderer."

"That's always been on the cards, hasn't it?"

"And that if Mr. X exists, we know two things about him."

And it was at that moment that Gibson suddenly retrieved his sense of humour.

"Do we? Can we deduce that he stood five feet nine and three quarters in his socks, had a wart over his left eye, and smoked only Benson and Hedges?"

"Let's leave all that to the clever buggers. What we can be sure of is that it was someone who knew his way about this house. And the garden, because he must have made—and previously planned—his escape by some back way. According to our showing he had thirty-six minus four, that's thirty-two seconds, which is quite a generous gap. But he wouldn't, of course, have wanted to push his luck. Well, anyway, it was someone who was confident about the premises. Secondly: what do we know secondly, Inspector?"

"That it was someone with whom Mrs. Bielby felt at ease. She was not even worried at seeing him in her bedroom."

"Perhaps. That's worth keeping an eye on. But what I was especially thinking was that it was someone who knew the ins and outs of Bielby's temperament. From the moment that Bielby left Mrs.

Fielding—from the moment he received his phone call, in fact—Mr. X was in remote but effective control of Bielby's every reaction. Oh—and there's one more thing—"

He went upstairs again without explanation, came down carrying the wedding photograph from the back bedroom.

"I propose to hang on to this for the time being."

"You think Mr. X might be on it?"

Gibson was beginning to learn that Kenworthy was not offended by irony.

"No, this is purely personal. I'm beginning to feel as if I know these folk rather well."

·7·

MRS. FIELDING WAS a woman a year or two over the forty mark. It might well be that in the last lap of potential fruition, she was attractive in a manner that had eluded her in her more inhibited younger years. There seemed something effortless, perhaps even unconscious, in the shapeliness of her figure. It might indeed have been effortless—perhaps even unconscious. But as a woman she might not have been every man's lure. Why specifically Bielby's? Her hair was prematurely grey; a slate grey which had as yet no marked inclination to whiteness, and was close-trimmed in geometrically satisfying curves that gave her, perhaps misleadingly, a vaguely academic air. She had hazel eyes that tried first to probe, and then to evade Kenworthy's. They must have looked in a very different manner on Bielby. Perhaps one day, when she had come to terms with her remorse and her present bewilderment had been diluted by familiarity, she would regain something that at the moment was difficult to define. She gave the impression of being far removed from her normal self; there seemed no guarantee that she ever would regain it. At bottom she was probably a much nicer person than Bielby had ever been.

John Henry Fielding was some fifteen years older than her, tall and spare, with a lot of hair that *had* gone white—a dirty grey-white. He did not attempt to conceal his hurt and perplexity, but he behaved like a man determined to do what seemed to be right, even if he scarcely understood why it should be right. He was in the house when Kenworthy called, having formed the habit since their domestic *débacle* of coming home for half an hour for his mid-morning coffee break: he was the third and now commanding generation that owned the largest furniture shop in the High Street. It might not be in order to spy on her that he now came rushing home at every available opportunity; nor even to consolidate their reconciliation. It might simply be to be with her, and to have her with him. That was the impression he gave. For there had been a reconciliation; it was common talk in Filton, and had been spelled out definitively for Kenworthy by Bartram. A rapid reconciliation had followed, apparently almost immediately, the discovery and confession of Lucette's perfidy. No one knew, of course, what the first twenty-four hours had been like, what a sleepless and separated night they must have spent. And now there was an awkward, not entirely fluent togetherness about the couple. Forgiveness, even quasi-saintly forgiveness, must surely have its unconvincing moments.

Lucy Fielding could be the sort of woman who for moral or sentimental or dogmatic reasons preferred to believe that she deserved her joy and pleasures. Perhaps, seen from Bielby's point of view, she had not been all that strange an aberration; but he surely must have been an inexplicable lapse for her?

"John Henry has been marvellous. He was stunned at first, of course. And then he asked me why. And it took him a little time to see that the reason I couldn't tell him was because I didn't know."

She closed her eyes, not in histrionics. She had been through a torment that she preferred to think she did not understand. She was not yet ready to believe that she was awake again from the nightmare. John Henry had, at his own suggestion—still meticulously doing all the right things—left Kenworthy alone to interview her. He had, in any case, to be getting back to his shop.

"I'm sorry I have to double-dig this ground," Kenworthy said. "Please don't think I enjoy prying. It's things of *material* relevance that I'm trying to unearth. You must pull faces at me if I get too near a sensitive nerve."

"The least I can do is try to help. Don't worry for my point of view, Mr. Kenworthy. You'll probably help me to get things into perspective."

"How long had you known Roger Bielby?"

"Known him? Well, all my life. Since I was in my teens and he began making his name in local politics. My husband has been a Borough Councillor the whole of that time, you know. But that's not what you mean by know him, is it? We first became closer friends about four months ago. And that started because we found ourselves on the same committee to raise funds for a disaster in Bangladesh."

"Bielby had been coming here, to this house, for four months?"

"Say three months. The first time he came, it was on committee business. I don't think now that it was entirely by accident that he always seemed to come when my husband was not here. John Henry has always worked his fingers to the bone on committee work, not only in the party and on the Council, but for the Church and the Chamber of Commerce as well."

"It was at about half past eight that Bielby came here on the night his wife was killed?"

"That is right."

"And what condition was he in?"

"Are you asking me to confirm that he had had too much to drink? And that he went on drinking after he got here?"

"That does not seem to be under dispute. Did he normally visit you in that state?"

"Certainly not—or he would not have been coming here. He was the worst for alcohol on the last two or three occasions: but never in the condition that he was in that night. I knew that if that went on, I was going to have to draw the line. I hadn't worked out how I was going to do it."

"You felt you had to be careful for fear of losing him?"

"I was under all sorts of delusions. I must have been out of my mind. I don't know how to explain it."

"For my part you don't have to. How long had he been drinking unusually?"

"Two or three weeks."

"For any reason that you know of?"

"I could see that he had something on his mind."

"His relationship with you, for example—and its complications?"

"No, not that. We had promised each other that we were not going to upset the *status quo* on either side. Mr. Kenworthy, I don't know how to make you see how much this was out of character."

"Yours or his?"

"Oh, God, Mr. Kenworthy—you must think I am shamelessly egocentric."

"Let's get back to his special worries. He didn't take you into his confidence?"

"I can see now that we hadn't grown as close to each other as all that. Roger could prattle on about personal things. But there were some subjects that I always knew he wouldn't talk about. There was a gap between us that, oh, I felt desperate to bridge—and that I knew I never would. And I'd have driven him away if he'd seen that I was trying. Then, as I say, this new worry came over him. I could see that it was eating into him. The drink wasn't helping. Sometimes he was far away."

"And you didn't try to coax it out of him?"

"I tried. But only in pleasantry. Just enough to see that it was hopeless. He could be a difficult man, Mr. Kenworthy. Not that I mean he was ever difficult with me. I suppose I was consciously steering clear of that sort of difficulty."

"But had you no clues? Nothing roused your suspicions? You must have evolved some sort of theory."

"Theory? Guesswork, rather."

"What then?"

"I thought there was something seriously wrong domestically."

"Because Mrs. Bielby was beginning to suspect what was going on here?"

"No, not that. I'm pretty sure it was not that. Margaret Bielby was too nice, too trusting. The sort of life that Roger and I were leading—well, it isn't too rare in the world nowadays, is it? Not that I'm offering that as any kind of excuse. But it was all far removed from Margaret's experience—even from her outlook."

"You make her sound either impossibly sheltered or impossibly deluded."

"I think she was both. She had a sort of stubborn innocence. That's all I can call it."

"You knew her well?"

"Scarcely at all."

"Yet you speak so categorically."

"She had twice been Mayoress. She had a public image. She was not guileful enough to cultivate a false one. Besides, Roger talked about her—a lot. She exasperated him, but he was fond of her. That was something he couldn't hide. It was just that she could not give him so much that he needed."

"So what sort of future did you foresee for the two of you?"

"We had none. We knew that. Haven't I said, we were not going to destroy the *status quo*?"

"Mrs. Fielding, did he ever talk to you about a woman in his past called Sally Carver?"

"No, never."

She looked genuinely puzzled.

Kenworthy looked up significantly at a hazy red crucifix, burning in a neon-tube in a wall shrine.

"Yours was a friendship that few people in Filton would have predicted."

"Oh, I know that as a younger man Roger had had

some bitter prejudices. There's a lot of bigotry in some of these Lancashire towns. And Roger had been the spokesman of an uncompromising faction."

"Until when? Until he got to know you?"

"He was mellowing, Mr. Kenworthy."

"And you must have been a real challenge to him. Tell me about this phone call, Mrs. Fielding."

"There's nothing I can tell you about it. The phone rang, and it was obvious from the start that whatever was being said was upsetting him."

"You're not going to tell me that it was him who picked the thing up when it rang?"

"As a matter of fact, he very nearly did. He was sitting nearest to it, and his hand went out automatically. I got there just in time. It could so easily have been John Henry."

"And you knew who it was who was calling?"

"Of course. She announced herself."

"In what frame of mind was his wife? Angry? Indignant?"

"Controlled. That's the only word I can think of. She just asked if she could speak to her husband; not even if he were here. Roger guessed a lot from the look on my face and simply took the receiver out of my hand."

"Could you hear anything of what was said?"

"Nothing at all."

"But you must have worked something out from the replies that he gave."

"Roger hardly spoke. I had the impression, I don't know why, that his wife had passed him on to someone else. All he said was noncommittal—and that he would be along."

"But he reacted afterwards?"

"He was livid. I know it sounds like a cliché: pretty well speechless with anger."

"How long did the conversation last?"

"Only a minute or so."

"Then?"

"Then he put down the phone, said 'the bitch—I shall have to go home.' I *have* told this to all the other inspectors—"

"I know. I just wanted to hear how you told it."

Kenworthy left the Fieldings' house and walked unhurriedly back to Bielby's, glancing at his watch as he went in at the gate. Four minutes: Inspector Heald had taken a lot of trouble over his chart.

Lorimer was back at his neighbourly task on the Bielbys' lawn, was in fact just turning his machine to set it at the last swathe. The busy little man signed with his head towards the back of the house. Inspector Gibson and his sergeant were at that moment coming out of the vegetable garden. There was no need for Gibson to announce what they had been doing.

"Anything?" Kenworthy asked.

"Stems of broad beans broken. A stray dog or a child might have done it. A pile of bamboo canes disturbed where they lie up against the back fence, one or two of them snapped. The fractures look recent. Could well have been somebody making a hurried exit."

"Overlooked at the back, is it?"

"No, we're on the edge of the moors here."

"Work out what routes Mr. X might have taken, and scout round for witnesses."

Gibson forbore to point out that that was just what he was on his way to do.

As Kenworthy was walking the gravel of the parking space, almost abreast of the front door, he was surprised to see someone come out of it: a strangely matched couple. The man, in his thirties, wore a sober grey suit with a slenderly knotted black tie. The woman could have been younger than him, but looked older: blonde-wigged, approaching the buxom, and with weak, full lips, accustomed to more enjoyment that they were getting at this moment. She was wearing black velvet, with a white blouse open at the throat.

The man had a markedly curved though smallish nose, and the vaulted forehead that left no doubt about his ancestry: except that contrary to the Leyland tradition he had an air of peevishness perpetually cleared for action. He looked at Kenworthy with self-righteous displeasure.

"I don't know who you are. I can hazard a guess, but you're not one I've met. Where do you think you are going with that?"

Kenworthy was still carrying in his hand, casually and unwrapped, the photograph of Mrs. Leyland's wedding group. The woman looked on without comment.

"Mr. Bielby Junior, I take it?"

The man nodded.

"And?"

"My sister."

"You live in Filton?"

"Thank God, no. This is our second visit over a short period of time. And I asked you a question."

"You are staying overnight? In this house? I ask, because I'd set great store by a little talk with you later."

"We are staying at the Bull."

"That will be most convenient."

"I still want to know, officer—I presume you *are* an officer?—what you are proposing to do with that photograph."

"I will give you a receipt for it. I would like to hang on to it for a day or two."

"Why on earth?"

"Montgomery used to cart Rommel's portrait about with him in his caravan. He found it a constant source of inspiration."

◆ 8 ◆

HEALD HAD COMPILED a schedule of Bielby's last hour:

0910   Person of Sidney Roger Bielby
            signed for at HM Prison, Preston,
            by Det.-Sgt. Underwood of Filton-
            in-Leckerfield. Also present PCs
            Dawkes and Hampson, Prison Of-
            ficers Wetherall and Saunders. Car
            a plain midnight-blue Cortina, un-
            marked as police vehicle. Bielby
            quiet.
0914   Party checked out at prison gates,
            PC Dawkes driving, Bielby in rear
            seat between Underwood and
            Saunders. Bielby unresponsive to
            small talk, make no effort to con-
            verse, but appeared to be taking
            interest in passing scenery.
0917   Vehicle left A6 south of Preston
            and proceeded by minor roads via
            Huntley, Gleave and Piper's End.
            This diversion ordered by DI Gib-
            son to evade press photographers.

0942	Vehicle slowed down by traffic at round-about north of Filton. Pulled into kerb fifty yards south of roundabout, when Underwood placed blanket over Bielby's head. Bielby compliant.
0943	Panda car crewed by PC Duckworth (driving) and DC Emerson pulled as prearranged into path of Cortina, which followed directly behind it for remainder of journey.
0945	Both cars halted by *ad hoc* traffic patrol (PC Harris) who held up oncoming stream to facilitate right turn into police station yard. Police Cadet Noble closed gate after entry.
0946	Car halted in yard. PC Saunders got out of offside rear seat and leaned inwards to attempt to remove blanket from Bielby. Manoeuvre proved difficult in enclosed space; Bielby told to get out first, helped by Saunders. DS Underwood got out of nearside door and came round car. Sergeant Booth (Sgt. Gaoler at Filton Hundreds Police Court) and PC Pasmore emerged from rear entrance to cells as reception committee.
0946.5	Bielby shot.

| 0951 | Bielby laid on stretcher brought by Sgt. Booth and PC Pasmore. Presumed dead. Body taken indoors. |
| 0956 | Clinical death confirmed by Police Surgeon S. R. Sterfield, M.D., B.Ch. |

The schedule said nothing of the things that had seemed impressive at the time: the crash of the rifle; the whiplash of the bullet fired diagonally down from a roof; Bielby buckling up; an obscenity of blood and filth; the struggle to get the blanket finally clear.

Superintendent Bartram was quickly on the scene: say by 0947. So were Kettle, Chief Inspector on day station duty, two cadets and two constables from behind clerical desks. Reverberations in the yard had been such that bystanders could not swear to the provenance of the shot. No flash had been seen, no gunsmoke. The only clue as to the direction from which it had possibly been fired was the way in which Bielby had been knocked back against the rear of the car at the moment of impact.

Bartram was quick to act. He decided at once that the roof or upper storey of the Tunnicliffes' warehouse, which formed one flank of the yard, was the most probable site of the ambush, and immediately despatched Chief Inspector Kettle with two constables to enter and search.

Secondly, he had radio messages sent to three squad cars on patrol in the Filton area, with a view to cordoning off check-points; not, as he said, that there was much hope, since an escapee, especially if he kept his cool, could easily get a long way away from

Tunnicliffes' in a very short time, without the need to use main thoroughfares. It would, on the other hand, have been irresponsible not to have taken the formal precaution.

Next he paraded in the yard for immediate duties all manpower available on the premises, leaving at their posts only those needed for minimal manning of switchboards, public office and crowd control in and near the courtroom.

Then he reported the incident to County HQ for coordination and direction of a wider task-force.

Finally, he called in from their rest days all traceable reserves in his division.

By 1020 the manned line round Filton was about 60% effective. By 1045 it was as strong as it could ever be hoped to be.

CI Kettle and his working party left the station by the front entrance to avoid reopening the yard gates. They therefore took fully five minutes to reach the front door of the Tunnicliffes' premises, arriving at about 0956. There was then considerable delay before they gained access to the builders' warehouse. The firm had ceased to trade about a month ago, being in financial straits. Kettle had just decided that the building must be unoccupied, and had divided his squad to search the surrounds, when the door was opened to him by William Tunnicliffe, the youngest (at 63) of the family. It took less than half a minute to brief Tunnicliffe about what had happened.

Tunnicliffe claimed to have heard no shot. Inspectors Gibson and Heald had later carried out their own experiments on this point, and both considered it admissible. The warehouse was a robust nineteenth-century conception. Sound travels upwards rather than downwards within buildings, and the room in which brother Herbert and sister Lois (both in their seventies) were making an inventory of stores to check against that made by the Official Receiver was three storeys under the roof, and situated towards the front of the building—i.e. at the furthest possible point from the police station yard.

Kettle and his crash force made straight for the upper floor, which was used for the storage of smaller items of builders' merchandise, much of it old, and a good deal of it unusable. The windows overlooking the police yard were extremely dirty and none of them could have been opened—or even touched—without leaving clear traces of disturbance. There was no such indication. Dust and festoons of cobwebs had not been molested. When Gibson carried out a more leisurely inspection, with a technical team later in the day, his attention therefore centred on the roof, which was reached by a trap-door above a length of fixed ladder. The bolts of the trap were closed (as Kettle had also found them) but well oiled and easily moved: the Tunncliffes said that this was a fire precaution. There were, however, no marks on the roof to suggest that the murderer had operated from here, though there were two possible spots from which he might have done. One was from the flank of a mansard window, the other from behind the base of a chimney cowl. Both places offered an unimpeded view across the yard, and at a range of about 120 yards would have afforded an unexacting target for a modest marksman with an efficient weapon. Of firing, how-ever, there was no evidence. The news came through

early that the bullet had been of .38 calibre, and
Gibson suspected a Luger mounted into a portable
shoulder-stock, perhaps in conjunction with tele-
scopic sights; all of which could be quickly disman-
tled and carried about the person. It was even possible
that the components had been discarded somewhere
about the warehouse itself, but there was so much
lumber in the place, some of it very heavy, that a large
force would have to be occupied for a very long time
to turn it all over: there was stuff here that had been
acquired in the Tunnicliffes' grandfather's day. Immediate search was necessarily fairly superficial; and
brought nothing to light.

Gibson paid particular attention to a door on the
first floor, which communicated with a simple block-
and-tackle hoist over the Tunnicliffes' yard: a verita-
ble puzzlegarden of chimney-pots, slates, bathroom
fittings and guttering. This door could easily be
opened from the inside, and was self-locking when
slammed from the outside. A man could have got out
of here, and crossed the yard comfortably in the time
it had taken Kettle and his small team to arrive. But
there were no traces of any such movement: the
ground was dry and had taken no recent imprints, and
nothing had been recently broken by the passage of a
man.

The Tunnicliffes' alibis were natural, undramatic
and supported each other. They had been working
together in the same room, checking their stock of
small fittings: William handling materials, Herbert
calling and Lois recording. They were all three of
them respected (though to some extent pitied) citizens

whose local standing went back to the eighteenth century.

Unpromising: Kenworthy sent his Sergeant Cooper to go over all the physical ground again, and Cooper came up with nothing more than Gibson had. So Kenworthy trod the attics and the roof on his own— and came up with nothing better. It must have been the shelter of either the mansard or the cowl; but there was not a cigarette-end, not a toffee-paper, not the impress of a sole on the lead. A disciplined man had done this. But then the sequence of events in Sandringham Avenue had been the result of disciplined thinking, too.

Kenworthy came downstairs and talked to the Tunnicliffe family, found them carefully formal at first, but gradually eased them into a gladness to be talking. He had done his homework about them with Bartram's help.

Herbert, the elder of the two men, was an autocratic bore, anachronistically and very noticeably the head of the family, with the other two well known never to argue with him beyond a certain point. He was paternalistic, and perhaps the other two needed a tribal figure in place of their own father; or else there was an effective agreement between the three of them never to let a difference grow into a quarrel. Certainly Herbert had made business mistakes in his time, for which the other two were believed to harbour him no grudges. Herbert managed the labour force and supervised operations in the field. William was, according to Bartram, a much more human and vivacious figure: a trim little man, not much more than five feet two inches in height, who liked his beer, was a

committee member of the Crown and Cushion Club,
and had charge of estimates, tenders and—in so far as
the Tunnicliffes tried to stay abreast of technological
progress—of developments and plant. Miss Tunnicliffe kept the day-to-day and annual books, pursued
debtors with waspish persistence and was in total
command of wages, PAYE and VAT.

It was Bartram's unequivocal view that the Tunnicliffes ought to have retired from the jungle of
business a decade and a half ago, while they still had
a credit balance and the vigour to enjoy it. They had
done badly in the adverse conditions of the last ten
years, but they were a family who set an old-
fashioned intrinsic value on the virtue of work for its
own sake. Despite costly credit, scanty mortgage
funds and insolvent debtors, they went on operating
as long as they thought they still had it in them to do
so, and probably harboured images of themselves as
the active octogenarians that the last two generations
of the family had been.

The opportunity therefore to tender for the St.
Luke's development—the Town Moor Shopping
Centre—had been a beacon on their horizon. They
could set it as a road to viability of credit and the
regeneration of their reputation. William's immense
task of estimating quantities bit heavily into their
diminishing reserves. But, thanks mainly to his modest final figures, based on unrealistically timorous
profit margins, they got the contract.

It was only after they had their footing on the site
of the old Playground that their problems really
started. They found themselves up against difficulties
such as their ancestors had never envisaged. Filton

Town Moor became one of the most notorious construction sites in the North-West. The Tunnicliffes'
greatly extended labour force included many who
were strangers both to the firm and the locality. There
were strong elements of subversive riff-raff, working
with more fits than starts; and even long-standing
servants of the family became infected by the con-
stantly repeated demands for solidarity in restrictive
practices. Three site foremen in succession suffered
accidents: a fall from scaffolding, an avalanche of
hard core, a runaway bulldozer. A rumour exploded
that Herbert Tunnicliffe's safety precautions were not
all they should be: the shop steward's whistle blew
again. Backlog had to be made up by crippling
overtime rates. There was vandalism at night. A
watchman was grievously injured; a security team had
to be brought in—and paid for. Two sub-contractors
withdrew, preferring to face a contractual penalty
rather than cumulative losses. A further rumor gained
currency that the Tunnicliffes were not going to be
able to pay their way—that those subcontractors still
left in the battle were going to have to whistle for their
next instalment, that even site wages were not assured
beyond another month. And pretty soon this was the
Tunnicliffe's reading of their own books. The bank
clamped down on extensions of credit and drew the
line for resettlement of existing loans. At the family
board meeting Herbert was grim but controlled,
Lois's lips were as tight as they were thin and (it was
remarkable how categorical Bartram could be about
the detail) there were actual tears in William's eyes.
They had to admit irredeemable failure. That had

been about three months before the first of the two murders.

Kenworthy came down from the roof and knocked on the half-open door of the room in which the Tunnicliffes were conferring. It seemed that their inventory of realizable assets had reached a stage of disastrous finality.

Kenworthy was received with an old-fashioned dignity. The Tunnicliffes were impressionable people; their attitude to dealing with a Scotland Yard figure was reminiscent of the thirties. Kenworthy's entrance struck them into a polite formality in which big brother Herbert had nothing to say, sister Lois even less; and little William was suppressed to a stage in which it was difficult to believe in the stories of his potential gaiety.

The first thing was to run over their alibi, which rested on the insistence of the trio that none of them had left one another's company for ten minutes on either side of the firing of the shot. They reiterated this, conscious of the gravity of their position. Should they come under actual suspicion, their support for each other could not be expected to carry much weight. Kenworthy tried to put them at ease by pointing out that as an experienced policeman he was always more impressed by an alibi that was obviously uncontrived.

"Of course," he said, "you must all have known Bielby well."

"Nobody earned his living in this town without knowing Bielby," William said. "But that doesn't mean we'd ever have invited him to dinner."

"I take it that you good people have done your own stint in local government too?"

No immediate answer. Herbert appeared to be looking a trifle uneasy. William spoke up for him. As the junior member of the family, he seemed suddenly ready to don the spokesman's cloak. Perhaps it was because as the merriest (in theory) of the family, he was considered the most appropriate link with the sophisticated world.

"Herbert did one spell on the Council," he said, "just after the war ended."

And now, that established, Herbert seemed to have gained the confidence to speak for himself.

"After that, I wanted no more of it."

"It must make a lot of inroads into a businessman's time."

"Too much talk. Altogether too much talk. Too much paper. And too much self-interest."

"This, of course, must have been before the arrival of Bielby on the scene."

"He came in at a by-election about half-way through my time."

"So you got to know him fairly well fairly early on?"

"He wasn't interested in getting to know me. He was a bumptious young caperer in those days."

"Was he ever anything else?" William asked.

"He did become a bit more approachable when he settled down."

"And what dealings did you have with him later on?" Kenworthy wanted to know.

There was an unexpected silence, an uneasy silence, as if this were the one question they were most dreading. Lois seemed to be taking great care not to be looking at anyone in particular. It was William who made the sudden move.

"Why don't we tell him?" he said.

He looked pertinently at Herbert, who held his eye for a solemn instant that was difficult to interpret. Lois kept herself primly aloof from the decision. William made it.

"You probably know already," he said, with a little forced laugh that Kenworthy ignored.

"Or put it another way. If you find out for yourself, you might jump to the worst of conclusions."

An argument for the vicarious persuasion of the others? Kenworthy waited.

"The point is this, Mr. Kenworthy: the chances of the small businessman in this town have got steadily worse as the years have gone by—and nobody's been in the mire quite as thickly as the building industry, what with the socialists going for a direct labour force and the big money investing in outside contractors. It got so there was nothing left for us except for the odd man who wanted to build his own house. And with the planning committee sitting on what they have the nerve to call green belts, there's only been one of those once in a blue moon. The last chance but one that might have come our way was the new Health Centre: and that went to a national company that hired the *Lump*. When the Town Moor job was put out to tender, we had to get it or bust. Literally. I'm not kidding, Mr. Kenworthy—we'd to win that contract or get out of business."

William was fluent now, his initial rigidity released by his new colloquial—and friendly—style.

"We'd have been better off if we had—got out of business, I mean. But we were not to know that. For the first time in our lives—and we were all agreed about it—my brother and I went to see Bielby."

He looked round at the other two for their agreement—not in fact so much for agreement as for accord with this confession. Lois was now staring ahead of herself; and of Herbert the least that could be said was that he registered no objection.

"We went to see Bielby at his home—this would be about four years ago—and we put it to him as Filtonians to a Filtonian: it was a question of survival, not only for us, but for those who depend on us—carpenters, bricklayers, labourers, electricians. And to our surprise, Bielby agreed with us. He said he had been trying to push things this way for a long time."

"Which was a lie," Lois said.

"It's all lies. Everything they do is all lies. You can't use the word *lie* any more. It's lost it's significance. What matters is cashing in on the last thing that was said. Bielby really did seem to see things from our point of view. He promised us we wouldn't have to worry this time."

"And how much did that cost you?" Kenworthy asked.

"Not a penny," Herbert intervened.

"Let's be honest, Herbert. We didn't have to cross his palm—as it happened. But we'd agreed, Mr. Kenworthy—"

He lifted his eyes and looked squarely first at his brother and then at Kenworthy.

"We'd agreed that if we had to break the rule of a

lifetime—of three generations' lifetimes—then, this time, it would have to be broken. It was the only way to survival. As I say, as it happened, such a thing never came into question. Bielby was in the right mood for a spell of local patriotism for a change. It suited his book to play that line both in the Council Chamber and the *Examiner*. Anybody would have thought he was a local saviour of a sudden. And he kept his promises."

William Tunnicliffe laughed humourlessly.

"Up to a point. We got the contract. So now there was a lot of snide talk in the corridors and ante-rooms that Tunnicliffe Brothers were not up to it. We were bound to fall down on the job. You'll have heard what happened: we did fall down on it."

William had got the bit between his teeth now and was no longer taking sidelong glances to check the reaction of his brother and sister.

"And if you're prepared to believe that it was all a series of accidents, Mr. Kenworthy, then I don't know why Scotland Yard employs you. You can see well enough how it turned out—and why it turned out as it did. It didn't worry Bielby putting us in the way of the Town Moor development, because he knew from the word go that it wasn't going to make an atom of difference. So Tunnicliffe Brothers were going to get the job. And the Forty Thieves, who've taken the rake-off from every construction job in Filton this last quarter of a century, can just bloody well wait for a year or two for a change. They'll get it in the end. And by then, Bielby and Co. can't be said to be favouring outsiders. They've given the family firm the chance it asked for—and see what happened.

Tunnicliffe Brothers are down the pan. The Town Moor has to be reallocated. The coast is clear for the Forty Thieves for the next decade. Never mind if a site foreman breaks his leg—or it might have been his neck—"

Herbert Tunnicliffe had been sitting through this outburst with his head bowed, ashamed of his brother's indiscipline, disowning its content. Suddenly he was no longer able to contain himself.

"Dangerous talk, William. You ought to know better. You know that neither you nor anyone else can prove a word of it."

"No. I can't prove a word of it. That's how it works, isn't it? Does it make it any the less true, because it can't be proved? You know damned well, Herbert, you think exactly as I do. You *know* the same as I do. Look at some of the unknown quantities we had to set on on that site. Look at some of the *known* quantities, the *local* bloody talent we had to end up with: a couple of Stringers, even a bloody Bennett—"

Herbert shifted in his chair as if some schoolboy had dusted the inside of his underwear with itching powder.

"Mr. Kenworthy—you mustn't take too much notice—"

"What's he bloody well here for, then, if not to take notice?"

"You spoke just now," Kenworthy said, "of some gentlefolk whom you referred to as the Forty Thieves. Would you care to name names?"

But even William Tunnicliffe saw the need for prudence here.

"Name names, Mr. Kenworthy? Do you think it's

as easy as that? Nominees: and the whole point of having nominees is that way no one can name names. The Forty Thieves is *our* name for a syndicate that's been putting the big things the way of the big boys. The law demands that a councillor declares his financial interest. But if his financial interest is in someone else's name—"

"This is all supposition," Herbert said, apologizing on his brother's behalf.

"Supposition, is it? All right, then—I'll name names. And Mr. Kenworthy can make what he likes of them. If there's anything to be proved, then let the professionals have the proving of it. I'll mention Roger Bielby for one, because he was the pivot of the whole operation. How do you think he ever got himself on to the Council in the first instance? He was nothing when he came to Filton: *nothing*. And if he hadn't made the right friends, he'd have stayed nothing. I'll mention Jeremy Hibbert, solicitor, as independent of politics as any man in Filton. Not Mawdesley's solicitor, oh no! Not for anything that's going forward in Mawdesley's name; but Bielby's solicitor. And how has he, an ex-grammar schoolboy in his first practice, made a quarter of a million in a quarter of a century? Not by defending bastardy cases in the police court. And not by any known connection with Mawdesley."

"You cannot bring Mawdesley into *this*, William."

This was Lois, inflexible and corrosive. "Mawdesley was in gaol the whole time we were working on the Town Moor."

"And do you think that a man like Mawdesley stops work just because he's in the cooler? With

Hibbert watching his interests? And Bielby still needing an income to live up to? Shall I also mention
Justin Hopwood, architect?"

"No, William. That's not fair. Justin has worked
for us."

Herbert was shouting now.

William laughed. "Or us for him. What's the
odds?"

He addressed himself to Kenworthy as if the other
two were not there, speaking softly, indignant empha-
sis in every syllable.

"Justin Hopwood, architect. Had some County
Council work seconded to him at a time when all the
permanent officials were up to their ears in work. He
designed a council house: a two-and-a-half bed-
roomed semi, with an all-purpose L-shaped room
downstairs. It was nothing very clever, had nothing to
distinguish if from anything else, except perhaps a
new kind of understairs cupboard. But the way
Hopwood's agreement was worded, he held the copy-
right on the plans, took a percentage royalty on every
copy that was put up. And they didn't go up in their
hundreds; they went up in their tens and hundreds of
thousands. Not only in this borough and this county,
but in opposite corners of England. Hopwood was a
rich man overnight; and the best of luck to him. He'd
done nothing dishonest, only been paid for his work at
several thousand times what it was worth. But how
come so many local authorities suddenly opt for this
very ordinary house? What sort of *quid pro quo*
influence is it that operates across county council
frontiers? Ask Hopwood how much of his royalty he
has to share with the Forty Thieves!"

The little man suddenly changed his tone.

"I'm sorry Mr. Kenworthy, I shouldn't be talking like this. A man ought to be jealous of his neighbours' reputations. Only I'm not. Not any more. I'm finished with codes and systems that make a man's honesty his most dangerous enemy."

"And you can give me good reason, can you, why the Forty Thieves should want to kill Margaret Bielby?"

The question brought William Tunnicliffe up short. It shocked him, transferring his fury to something pathetic and real. He was red in the face, short of breath from emotion. But Kenworthy's tone of voice jolted his thoughts to a different plane. He collected himself for an instant.

"No, I can't, Mr. Kenworthy. That's a fact, I can't. Why anyone should want to kill Maggie—"

Even at this interval from the event, words were still failing him.

"That's something about which we all feel the same," Herbert said, with what in his dour discipline amounted to heartfelt sincerity.

"You knew her well, I take it?"

"We did. Well enough to know what she was up against."

This was William again, registering a wholly different kind of anger, but still with the threat of outrageous indiscretion in his voice, if that should seem to help the case.

"I didn't know her before the war, but Herbert did, because Tunnicliffe Brothers had the maintenance contract on the Town Moor when the Mawdesleys were the landlords."

"Maintenance contract!" Herbert sneered. "That means we weren't called in for a house that was merely falling down. If it was likely to take half the row with it, we might be called in to do a spot of repointing."

"The Town Moor estate was originally built to house workers in the Prince Consort Mill," William explained unnecessarily.

"So I did visit number twelve, Elgin Row, once or twice," Herbert went on, as if there had not been an interruption. "Enough to see that neither Maggie nor her mother belonged on that scrap-heap."

"And I went there after the war," William said. "When the Bielbys first married, before they got their house in Sandringham Avenue, they went on living for a few months on the Town Moor. I can't describe to you the state that property was in. They had to change the bedroom wallpaper once a month. That was the state of the rising damp. Bielby asked for an estimate to make the place more habitable: nothing on a grand scale, you understand. For one thing, Bielby couldn't have afforded it in those days. And for another, the property wasn't worth a bad penny. But we did a bit of relining, cleaned out some of the guttering. And I remember calling one morning, to see how things were going—Herbert was out on a job somewhere else—and I could see that Maggie had been crying. I could see it was not just a sentimental weep about something or other. It was a real upset. It would be about half past nine, and Bielby was out at work, and it looked to me as if they'd had a bad breakfast time. I never did find out what it was all about. Of course, she pulled herself together as soon as she saw me on the doorstep."

"But you never knew Bielby in the days when he was Wheeler?"

"There was no chance of that, Mr. Kenworthy. You have to understand that the Town Moor was rough in those days. If we went there to work, with a gang, on a lorry, then that was all right. And we're not snobs, at least. I hope we're not, not by any yardstick. But it wouldn't have been *safe*, Mr. Kenworthy, for a stranger in those days to go up Swallow Street alone."

"More credit to Bielby for hoisting himself out of it, then."

"You have to give him that. It's what he did with himself after he'd finished hoisting that was the trouble."

"So tell me this: who gave him his first chance? I mean, his breakthrough into finance and politics? Not the editor of the paper, surely?"

"No. Old Jethro was straight as a die."

"And he did it independently of the major political parties?"

"He made friends with Mawdesley, Mr. Kenworthy. One minute they were fighting like tomcats over the first offer for sale of the Town Moor. The next, they'd become friends behind everyone's back."

Kenworthy looked at the other two to see what confirmation or supplementary information might be forthcoming. But Herbert had relapsed into his long-faced, uncommunicative mood. And Lois, who had scarcely said a word the whole time that Kenworthy had been in the room, was now looking as if the whole discussion had been a lemon that she had been sucking. The moment he left them, it was certain that William was going to find himself in opprobium with his partners.

Kenworthy sat in Superintendent Bartram's office, toying with the foulest cup of coffee that had ever come out of a police canteen.

"Tell me about the Stringers and the Bennetts."

"Which generation? Those out of Bielby's golden past?"

"No. Those that the Tunnicliffes employed on the Town Moor site."

"Same ilk: grand-children, nephew's kids. Tear-aways, the same as those that Bielby kicked about with in his Wheeler days. 'I found it in my pocket, Mr. Bartram. I don't know how it got there. Some-body's trying to fix me.'"

"The bottom must really have dropped out of the Tunnicliffes' barrel."

"It had. They tried for one short spell to set this squad of non-union labour to clear up some of the damage. It didn't last more than a week."

"Were the Stringers and Bennetts behind the aggro on the Tunnicliffes' site?"

"They hadn't the brains."

"But the muscle?"

"Anybody needing Stringer and Bennett muscle would have been out of the game a long time ago. Out of all games."

"Are you a native of Filton-in-Leckerfield, Super-intendent?"

"No. Rossendale. Different sort of valley; but not so you'd notice. We had our playgrounds, too."

"You seem so familiar with ancient history here."

"I did a spell here as a sergeant, 'way back in the fifties."

"So you can tell me something about Mrs. Bielby's half-brother, the one they call Cliff."

"I arrested him myself—twice. Do you want the file, or will memory do?"

"Just a sketch, for the time being."

"Just another bloody cowboy, going the way Sid Wheeler was; perhaps with a spot more dedication. Ingenious, ambitious—and something that Bielby never was: *cold*. It was ironical that Bielby should have been the one to try to take him in hand; not that Bielby cared a monkey's fart, once he'd made sure of Maggie. We picked Cliff up on a breaking and entering job, not more than a month or two after his mother died. But you know what a juvenile court's like: first offence and the benefit of a trick-cyclist. And Bielby, already the rising star of the *Examiner*, standing up in court like a Sunday-school teacher. 'I'd like your Worships to know that I shall be keeping an eye on the boy.' That was all Maggie-bait in those days, of course. But the second time, it was Bielby who shopped him to us, behind Maggie's back. And he still played both ends against the middle and won both games. He stood up and pleaded for Cliff in open court; at the same time he'd had a quiet word with the bench, who by this time were pals of his."

"When was this?"

"I can get you chapter and verse. Break-in with GBH, the second time, and Cliff had older men than himself working for him. He got Borstal."

"Recidivist? Where is he now?"

"I don't know. And as long as it isn't Filton-in-Leckerfield, I'm happy. For all I know, he may even have gone straight. It has been known—they tell me. I heard from somewhere that they'd trained him as a motor-mechanic. It might have appealed to him. He didn't come back here—perhaps by then he'd grasped which side his bread *wasn't* buttered. At any rate, we haven't even had a query about his old days. You're digging a lot of cross-cuts, aren't you?"

"I've got a gut-feeling we're going to go back thirty years for the answers to a lot that's been troubling us. Now I'd like to know a lot more about Mawdesley."

"You've got time on your hands, have you? It took the DPP eighteen months just to read the evidence. And that was after the county fraud squad had had God knows how many men working on the case for two years."

"I'll work from a digest. I'll go and see him, too."

"I think you'll like him. Everybody else did. He was a very generous soul. Mind you, you can afford to be, when you've hived off half a million. I'm not kidding, Kenworthy, it was not a penny less: and that's only counting what was known about. Of course, nowadays he can't quite keep up the standards he used to. Otherwise he'd be drinking a lot more than he does. Just to increase his misery, his wife divorced him while he was inside. And of course, much though we all like him, there's never been any serious thought of his readmission to the Crown and Cushion Club. It wouldn't do, would it—even though it was him who gave them four new billiard tables and bought the steward's house for them when the lease fell in. That's the sort of man he was; open-handed, you might say—in both directions. He gave so much—that he'd pinched—towards the building of the new Church of England Secondary School—that they were going to name it after him. *The Francis Mawdesley Secondary School:* carved in letters three feet high over the front door. They had a hell of a job, refacing the masonry—and they dared not even start on the job until after both trial and appeal. However: some people have to stay above reproach, and I never did hear that the Church had given thirty thousand back to the Prince Consort shareholders. It's a pity we didn't leave him at large a year or two longer. He might have paid for the new police station."

·9·

MAWDESLEY LIVED IN a large Victorian villa that stood
in surprisingly extensive concealed grounds not a
stone's throw from the centre of the town. It was not
perhaps an imposing mansion for a man who com-
manded the funds that he had once lavished. But it
represented affluence by the standards of his
nineteenth-century forbears, and the Prince Consort
Mills had always stood substantially as a family
concern. Patronage was organically in Francis
Mawdesley's bloodstream.

The garden was neglected. Dusty, scraggy weeds in
the gravel of the drive, straggling rhododendrons and
sere heads of lupins standing amongst tall grasses to
denote what had once been a flower bed.

The same spirit reigned inside the house. There
were dust sheets over the furniture in some of the
downstairs rooms—a gap where a whole suite had
gone missing. Flogged for Scotch? Mawdesley
seemed to be living largely in what had once been a
breakfast-room: a single-bar electric fire was standing
askew on the hearth rug. It was difficult to believe
that his material poverty was as dire as it looked.

Surely he had had something cached in reserve? His
present surroundings had the look of a self-imposed
poverty of the spirit. And he answered the door
himself: a balding man in his late sixties, his head
trimly cropped, as if that were a habit that he could
not jettison. He was wearing an incredibly drab
chocolate-brown sweater.

To quote a telling phrase from the prosecution, his
offences had been contrived by methods not readily
apparent under the normal practices of audit. That
was how the accountants had covered up their own
purblindness. His principal skill had been the raising
of orthodox loans and against non-existent securities.
In the largest of all his operations, these securities had
taken the form of stock held for marketing in warehouses whose shelves actually stood empty. For
whereas books can be cross-checked, not all potential
creditors think actually to walk round stockrooms. An
irony of the closing stages of the Mawdesley case was
that he had paid so much tax on profits that he had
declared but never made that the ultimate rebate made
to his creditors by the Inland Revenue ran into several
thousands. And there had been a certain naive simplicity in Mawdesley's orthodoxy. Most of his
gains—they did actually tip the scale, as Bartram had
said, at £500,000—had been made at the expense of
one of the High Street banks; whose branch manager
was nevertheless totally exonerated, since all the
wrong decisions had been made at a very high level
indeed.

But there was no sign of his signal successes in
Mawdesley's present setting. Hospitable by nature, he
offered to make Kenworthy a pot of tea, but in such a

tone of deep fathomed weariness that it would have been an unkindness to have put him to the trouble. Mawdesley was tired, disillusioned—and bored. He was even without a television set, the aerial cable lying dustily coiled against a skirting-board. A novel—historical romance by some woman or other—was lying open across the arm of a chair, but it was doubtful from his general miasma of fatigue and incuriosity whether he was even capable of the continuity of reading.

"You wanted to talk to me, Chief Superintendent?"

"About Roger Bielby."

"A fearsome business. Two fearsome businesses. I don't see how I can help you."

"I've heard it said that you're the one who put him on his feet when he first came here."

"Somebody has been making use of his imagination."

It was difficult to picture Mawdesley as the fashioner of civic destinies. There was a scrawniness about his neck that had once been the backup to a double chin; a certain sagging character about a lower lip that had once been set in determination. His eyes were lustreless; but his sophistication had once been selective. He had once collected Alvis cars. He had owned a yacht in the Bahamas, a villa in Marbella.

Kenworthy had talked around about Mawdesley after leaving Bartram, had read files in the *Examiner* office. The biggest splash in Mawdesley's life had been his daughter's wedding: on the very eve of the opening of the investigation of his affairs. She had married big Canadian money, and he had matched his sterling against their dollars. The reception had rivalled anything the Lord Lieutenant had ever mounted for visiting royalty. The couple's honeymoon was said to have cost him fifty thousand, and it was that that had set him on his last-fling credit operation.

Since then he had queued up to empty his urinal bucket. He had made balsa wood aircraft in his cell. He had paraded in front of the Assistant Governor and asked permission to keep a pet canary. There had been some cruel whispering because he had served most of his sentence in a low-security prison where the deprivation might have been more stringent; and that largely in the presumably congenial company of other erstwhile financial magicians. What he had lost had never been his by right; but could it be true that he had lost it all? The final deficit had been such that the Prince Consort Mill had paid out less than twopence in the pound; and there was not a creditor who wasn't hoping for more. Surely Mawdesley had something somewhere? Could he have been so bumptious that he never imagined himself in these straits? What sort of a settlement had his wife made away with? (There had been a woman or two but, it seemed, Brenda Mawdesley had played a calculated tolerance until it became clear that there was nothing left, even for her.)

It was possible to feel sorry for Mawdesley to some extent. As Bartram had said, the leading lights of the town had liked him, still did, though it fell short of readmitting him to their inner circles. His trickery had been grotesquely impudent; he must have ruthlessly trodden into the ground any opposition that realistically threatened him. But there was a complete absence in him of anything that he would have recognized in himself as malice. He had stolen to give away; and if pride had been the motive for that, it was giving itself that had become the habit and the joy.

All this it was possible for Kenworthy to think as he looked at the fallen Mawdesley. And it was not the material fall that had to be pitied: it was the clouded eyes, the ebb of ambition, the sapping of the spirit. Kenworthy ploughed on.

"If Bielby, as a young sub-editor and local feature-writer had had his own way to make in a town in which he had been a juvenile delinquent, it would have taken him ten years at least to make the Borough Council—if ever at all."

"So someone gave him a leg-up. It's only when the dog has cleared the stile that some people can see that he isn't lame."

This was Mawdesley's first attempt at self-justification, and there was even a hint of rising energy behind it; but on balance, it was a surly defence.

"Bielby was the medicine Filton needed. He was the medicine this country needed. He and his type are the medicine England needs now. Anyone could see that. You had only to read the first editorial he ever wrote for the *Examiner*."

"What was that about?"

"A compulsory purchase order on some land the County Council wanted for more bloody offices. He had no room for cosseting the namby-pamby. All that can do is swell the ranks of the self-pitiers. Christ, we got to the stage where we had to have a working party to decide where to put the saucer of milk for the office cat. *Profit* had become the dirtiest word in the English

language. Could these silly sods not see that if
individual firms were not making a profit, the country
as a whole must be running at a loss?"

Mawdesley had not talked his mind for a long time;
it was a muddle of the clichés and catch phrases of his
working life. And he took for granted a lot of
agreement from a man he considered intelligent.
Kenworthy expressed no opinions.

"How the hell can the country prosper if private
enterprise is shackled?"

Private Enterprise as Mawdesley had understood
and operated it? Had the man an ethical tenet in his
mind? Three and a half years inside—and did he
believe in himself that he hadn't committed any
crime?

"So you saw Bielby as the manner-born spokesman
of all you believed in?"

"Anyone could see he was the man of the moment
as far as Filton-in-Leckerfield was concerned."

"I'm interested in the mechanics of it."

"The mechanics of what?"

"Getting him his first seat on the Council, before
he'd been in the town more than five minutes."

"I don't see that that has any relevance to what's
happened in the last month."

"Maybe it hasn't. Yet maybe it has. I'm like a man
doing the biggest jigsaw puzzle in the North West
without the original picture to copy from. I don't even
know what the picture was."

"It won't help to go digging up the forties and
fifties. And in any case, I don't see why you come to
me about it. I've never sat on Filton Council in my
life. Or on any other council either, for that matter."

No, of course; he hadn't had to. He'd had other people sitting for him: the likes of Bielby.

"Bielby got on through his own ability."

"Once the talent had been spotted."

"Well, I'm no political talent spotter; never have been."

"But you did befriend Bielby in his early days."

"Is that a crime, then? Kenworthy—I've served what I owe—"

Sooner or later he had had to say that; they all did. Kenworthy let him work it out for himself. A man of Mawdesley's fortunes and record could not but be ill at ease to receive any kind of visit from the police.

"Friendship's no crime," Kenworthy said, sweetly reasonable. "But I've been looking up back numbers, and my reading is that Bielby won his first seat in Lower Heathside Ward by a walkover after he'd been in Filton a year, the Conservative candidate having withdrawn his papers a week before the election."

"Not a Conservative candidate. There are no Conservatives as such on Filton Borough Council—or at least, there weren't in those days. They sat as Independents. It was the Socialists who introduced politics into local government in this part of the world."

"I dare say. That isn't what interests me. I'd like to know why Councillor Beavis was so ready to stand down."

"That's easy. Nothing sinister about that. Ted Beavis's wife was in the middle of a difficult pregnancy."

"And he got back on the Council the next time round?"

"That's right."

Mawdesley seemed to brighten up at having the answer provided for him.

"He did the right thing to put family first."

"And he was, after all, Filton's next mayor."

"As it happened. There's always been a shortage of men of the right ability who can afford to take time off from their businesses."

"And Bielby became the most active undercover nonmember that the Independents ever had?"

"It's not fair to say that. He was a pain in the neck to them half the time. Some thought he was the best undercover member the Socialists ever had."

"I'm sure he was. That was part of his strength, wasn't it? But I'll bet he jumped into action when some people shouted."

"Listen—you didn't know Bielby. He was a bloody handful, and, like most of us, he took a lot of handling in his younger days. If you're suggesting that he was somebody's puppet, then you're clueless as to what sort of man he was. The man didn't live who could make Bielby speak, vote or act in a way he didn't believe in."

No; there must have been a few serious scenes, before Bielby had got the hang of it. But once they got him a mortgage that was too big for his salary and his rake-off, he would have to start looking where the next bonus was coming from.

No use to browbeat Mawdesley about what the payoffs had been, and how they had been managed. He would give nothing away, and Kenworthy knew he had not the leverage to force it out of him. There was no point in putting him even more aggressively on the defensive.

"Have you seen Bielby since you were discharged, Mr. Mawdesley?"

"For two minutes, on a tobacconist's doorstep."

"They didn't think of throwing you a coming-out party, then?"

Mawdesley looked at Kenworthy with disgust and contempt.

"Kenworthy, it's all very easy for you. You know what you know, and you think all the wrong things that I know you must be thinking. All right, you're thinking a few of the right things, too. I'll concede you that. I gave a lot of bloody money away in this town. Never mind for the moment where it came from. I put a lot of poor sods on their feet. And there are even more that I set a head and shoulders higher than they ought to bloody stand. And I'm not without my feelings. Listen, Kenworthy: I'd been home about a month and I was shopping round the market, and I happened to pick up a cauliflower from a stall, weighing it in the palm of my hand. And I saw a plainclothes detective take a step forward behind me. Because as far as he was concerned, I was just a plain thief. And even that's better than being forgotten. Even *forgotten* is the wrong word for it. There are men in this town who wish they could forget me— who pretend that they can."

"Bielby amongst them."

"Bielby's dead."

"So is his wife," Kenworthy said softly.

"And that is something that I don't understand. That's a side of the question for which I would happily tear this bloody town down, if I thought I could be an ounce of use to you."

"As far as I can tell, that's how *everyone* feels about her."

"She deserved someone a bloody sight better than Roger Bielby, and that's for certain. And when I say that, I'm not getting at *him*. He was what he was—as I am what I am, and you are what you are. But he was the wrong man for that lass from the Town Moor."

Mawdesley paused to compose himself.

"I remember once giving him the telling-off of his life—ripped the bugger into shreds. And that was because of the way he treated his wife."

No lack-lustre to his eyes now.

"It was not all that long after they were married, and only a few weeks after they had moved into Sandringham Avenue. Bielby thought he knew his way about the world. He thought he was Filton's consultant on high living. All he knew on that score, he'd learned in an air force mess. But he was for ever picking at Maggie for the things that she didn't know, couldn't know—things that he didn't always get right himself, anyway. And even in front of his guests, he'd show her up; if he didn't actually say anything, he'd look round the table as if he were apologizing for her. This particular night, it had to do with the chilling of a wine. She'd stuck a full-blooded Burgundy into the fridge until she put it on the table. And half the other ignorant sods that he had there wouldn't have noticed, wouldn't have known any better themselves. But he had to make a little scene out of it. I could see the hurt in her face. And when she came back from a trip to the kitchen between courses, I could see that she'd had her little weep. I got him on one side before we went home, and I tore into him as I haven't torn into many men in my life."

"There are some who would say, of course, that she should never have stood for it. It was her own fault if she put up with it from him."

"That's not knowing Maggie. She was made what she was made: too nice for Bielby. And married to him in front of an altar. That sort of thing mattered to her."

"But they did make some sort of go of their marriage?"

"Then there were the children," Mawdesley said. "Bielby had always had a thing—a very strong thing—about broken homes. I think he believed that his own life would have been in some way miraculously different if he had had a normal childhood."

I think he believed—

In Mawdesley's somewhat bulbous eyes there was an ingrained satisfaction with himself, an inability to question his own standards. Bielby had been a different kind of man from him, and anyone different was inferior to Mawdesley; even in his present condition.

"But the Bielbys had had their children off their hands for some time, surely?"

"Old habits die hard—even uncomfortable ones. Surely you as well as I, Kenworthy, have known warring couples who will go on for ever because that's what they've always been used to."

"In any case, I don't suppose there'd ever been anything like this Fielding affair while the fledgelings were still in the nest."

Kenworthy's remark was intended not as a statement, but as a cue for revelations. But Mawdesley simply shrugged. The occasional excitements outside the bounds of his marriage had been part and parcel of his existence. They might have needed tactical management, but had not involved struggles with conscience or preconditioning.

"None of us believed that Maggie could give him all he wanted on that side of life," he said.

"There *were* other adventures, then?"

"As far as a man can be sure, I'd say not."

Qualified, but a confident, once-and-for-all assertion, nevertheless: Kenworthy looked at him for development of the theme.

"What you have to understand, Kenworthy, was that Bielby was no ordinary man: he was a highly contradictory man. But all his views were strong ones, even those that seemed to clash with one another. He was very fond of Maggie."

"So fond of her that it's unthinkable that he should have shot her?"

Mawdesley shrugged again.

"I don't think that fondness has anything to do with that," he said.

Jeremy Hibbert had none of that deed-box-and-mahogany solidity that one might have associated with a Lancashire solicitor: no shelves of comprehensively ancient Statutes. His expanse of desk, topped with engine tooled green leather, was bare of anything but two telephones and a casually lying silver ballpoint pen. A one-way glass set into his door enabled him to keep a godlike eye on his surprisingly large typing pool—six girls, rattling away on electric typewriters in the outer office.

Hibbert, a man at the lower border of his fifties, had contrived to give himself what looked, at some angles, like a positively grotesque illusion of youth. It derived from a profuse head of vintage Beatle-cut—now almost twenty years out of fashion. He received Kenworthy with a convinced though not actually discourteous air of his own superiority. He waved Kenworthy to a chair and produced for him an ashtray—with all the suppressed contempt of a man who had no use for such things himself. Kenworthy made no move to smoke, but explained his business.

"Not," Hibbert said, "that I imagine I can be of much use to you."

"The story goes that you had a vital difference with Bielby about the line of his defence."

Hibbert preserved a thin lipped silence, ham-acted but not jocular.

"Not," Kenworthy said, "that I'm seeking anything for the record."

"I would hardly have thought, Chief Superintendent, that you were a man who needed instruction in the relationship between solicitor and client."

Kenworthy got up at once from his chair and responded with a provocatively faint and friendly smile.

"That's what I expected you to say. And it's been worth the twenty minutes' wait for the sake of hearing you say it."

He got to the door and opened it before Hibbert could do it for him. Then, leaning on it half-open as he went through it, he spoke in a voice that could be overheard by the typists.

"I only asked you because I thought that perhaps

Bielby wanted to press the most effective defence of all."

Hibbert looked at him from behind a facade of amused impassivity.

"You see, I think Bielby wanted to shelter behind the fact that he knew who *had* killed his wife."

· 10 ·

THEY WERE TAKING their coffee at the remotest corner table in the residents' lounge of the Bull when Kenworthy came up after his own dinner. The omniscient Bartram had filled him in about them.

Roger John Bielby was thirty-one, had been to a minor public school, had a campus university arts degree and had followed it by common or garden training in accountancy. He was now a featureless executive with a multi-national company in Bracknell, had two children of his own and rarely came to Filton-in-Leckerfield. He had all the facial characteristics of the Leylands, Maggie and her Mum; but none, it seemed, of their sympathy with mankind.

His sister, three years younger, had gone to teacher training college, which she left after one year for marriage with a man called Travis, of whom her father disapproved. So, pretty soon, did she, for they had split up after less than eighteen months. She still lived in Leeds, where the marital home had been. From the mock-up bib-and-brace boiler suit that she was wearing tonight it was difficult to judge her state of affluence. And eye shadow, false eyelashes and an off-blonde wig made it difficult to be sure which side of the family she resembled. It would have been uncharitable to describe her as raddled, but she looked as if she were going to be raddled before many more years had passed. She probably smoked and drank at least a little to much, slept not quite enough, ate some of the wrong things, and a trifle too irregularly. Her brother was peaky, hypercritical of the standard views of whatever group he found himself in at any given moment, yet had nothing of his own to substitute for whatever ethos he was knocking down. Megs looked (and sounded to Kenworthy in such conversation as he was able to overhear) warm-hearted in a merely sentimental way, without either originality or staying power.

Kenworthy contrived his entrance soft-footedly and obliquely behind the pair, so that for a couple of minutes they were not aware that he was in the otherwise deserted residents' lounge. He went over to sift through a pile of periodicals on a side table. The pair appeared to be disagreeing in a nonchalant way about the integrity of their late father, whom the girl was defending with the loyalty of habit.

"At least there's his service record. You can't deny he was a brave man at the time."

"Brave? What's a brave man? Too scared to do the sensible thing for fear of what people might say? Brave? You could call it weak-minded."

"I'd like to see you fly one of those rackety planes night after night through all that anti-aircraft fire."

"In the close proximity of three or four other men

who were ruthlessly watching your every reaction? There was another of his RAF tales that always seemed to me nearer the mark."

His sister took a cigarette from a packet that was lying in front of her as if its very presence on the table was a comfort to her.

"I remember he told the story one Christmas when we were kids, and our Uncle Cliff had come over and they'd both given the port a fair bashing. It was all about how he'd won some stupid baton of honour for square-bashing in his elementary training days. It seems there was a flight sergeant drill instructor whose word was law, and who'd stay in camp all night boning up recruits' equipment for them at a shilling a time. He was on to a winner, because anyone on morning parade whose webbing hadn't been blancoed by him was likely to be docked points for his turnout. Some of the squad decided that this kind of blackmail was not exactly what they were fighting the war for, so they got up a deputation to the squadron commander, of which Dad was supposed to be a member. Only he sneaked out of it at the last moment. And the Squadron Leader treated any protesting recruit as a bolshie. On the night before the passing-out parade, Dad was the only one who passed any more money to the Flight sergeant. And he won the day, which rings truer to me than the variations on how he won his medal."

Kenworthy chose that moment to intrude on their line of vision, and they stopped talking in a mixture of guilt and irritation. When his coffee tray was brought, he invited himself to join them in a manner which even Roger John would have found difficult to repulse. He stayed with them an hour and a half, questioning them unobtrusively about their family life and childhood routines. It was an exploration of the character of the children rather than of their parents. He attempted hardly any analysis of pre-murder events. And the pair tended to do their best to agree with each other in the face of such a redoubtable reputation as Kenworthy's. They were loyal to their background and revealed little that could have contributed to one of Inspector Heald's charts. Nevertheless, Kenworthy pressed on, despite the fact that the colleagues he had brought from London were spinning out modest drinks in the neighbouring bar, where they were waiting for an operational conference he had called for an hour ago.

Then as he finally pushed himself away from the table and made ready to go, young Bielby remembered another source of bile.

"By the way, I've a complaint. A bag of golf clubs: missing from the house since you people took over."

"Since we took over? Since you last set eyes on them, don't you mean? When was that?"

"When I was last in the house. About a year ago, I suppose."

"Well, I can account for them—"

Kenworthy lied fluently.

"They were retained for forensic examination. I'm not exactly sure why: you'll understand that a lot of wrong trails have to be followed up in a case like this. I'll have them brought round here for you in the morning."

"Thank you."

But there was no gratitude in it: it was a puerile

innuendo that, but for his vigilance, Roger John might never have seen those clubs again.

"They are extremely valuable," he said. "My father had them custom-made for me, and I'm thinking of taking the game up again."

"I'm glad to hear it," Kenworthy said.

· 11 ·

KENWORTHY SWEPT INTO the Bull's American Bar with
the bluster of a man who has been frustrated beyond
tolerance. He behaved, in fact, as if it was he who had
been kept waiting. And his team followed him breath-
lessly up the stairs, which he took two treads at a
time. But then, when they reached his bedroom, he
despatched them all off to fetch their tooth-glasses.
He had a half-bottle of John Haig, and produced it as
if it was a wild party that he was proposing for the five
of them: golden spirit drunk out of the squashy blue
plastic, with water splashed in, for those who wanted
it, from the wash-basin tap.

There was not enough space for a conference in the
long, narrow, single-bedded room. He had the two
sergeants perch on the edge of his bed. Pasty Morley,
shorthand pad at the ready, settled herself on the
windowsill. Kenworthy took the single comfortless
armchair. Inspector Heald slipped back to his room
for his own chair.

Kenworthy's room was littered with bits of *per-
sona:* including faded blue pyjamas that looked as if
the last hint of colour would be drained out of them in

the next wash. It was rather surprising to see that his
bedtime reading appeared to be George Eliot. The single
artistic solace provided by the hotel (an abstract based
on pithead gear, painted with imitation ceramic effect)
had been taken from its hanger and now stood against
the wall, sideways on. In its place he had hung the
Leyland wedding photograph: happy, self-conscious,
impoverished respectability, grouped round the front
door of 12, Elgin Row.

"Now—"

All day long he had had his minions out in the
town: not with a door-to-door questionnaire, not with
key questions; not even advertising their identity,
which might have offended the sensibilities of some
of the potential sources.

"For God's sake don't try to be scientific," he had
told them. "We've got time on our hands—at least
you have. So let's enjoy luxury; let a few ideas drift in
to us."

Polite, disciplined, and all to some extent scared of
him, they had avoided catching one another's eye in
his presence. *Intuition* was a dirty word in modern
detection.

"The moment you put a suggestion into anyone's
mind, you can consider you've failed. What I want is
spontaneity. I want to know what people are thinking—
not what they'd like us to think they are thinking."

He had sent them out to strike up conversations, in
parks and the marketplace, told them to join in the
slowest queues in the supermarket check outs, in the
hope that the collective soul of Filton-in-Leckerfield
would slip some undervalued triviality.

He had sent Sergeant Cooper, the progressive

romantic, round the lounge bars and the more exclusive shops, playing the casually inquisitive stranger, dropping stones to start ripples in pools.

"If you find a man behind the counter of a high-class tobacconist's who has a Rotary or Round Table badge in his lapel, get him talking about how the police are dragging their feet."

Sergeant Widgeon, true blue, four A-levels and a taste for Henry James, he had sent round the council estates, pretending to do market research into the efficacy of television advertising.

"Give at least half the day to the tower block on Coldsprings. You might even find someone who used to live on Swallow Street."

Inspector Heald, who had suppressed comment while these chores were being propounded, he had left to his own devices. That, he said, would guarantee the random element.

"You can see what kind of thing I'm after. Serendipity: which the dictionary defines as the faculty for making felicitous finds."

Pasty Morley's pencil hit the pad as soon as Sergeant Cooper started to describe his day.

"Of course, sir, you'll understand that this is all hearsay."

"Of course it's hearsay. Hearsay's our only possible source at this stage. This isn't a court of law, Sergeant. It's justice we want to see done."

"Well, sir, after I'd been going an hour, I came to the conclusion that this is the tightest-lipped town I have ever been in—and the most charitable. You'd think they'd adored the Bielbys. He'd been a public benefactor. What hadn't he done for Filton! And his wife was a sort of mythological mother-figure."

"Exactly the feeling out on the estates," Widgeon interrupted. "Except that when I probed deeper, I found all sorts of half-conscious reservations hedging round Bielby himself. But Maggie survived every round."

"Precisely my finding," Cooper said.

"Twice she was mayoress, and she seemed to have done the job with something a little deeper than the common touch, a sort of *durable* common touch. A woman I spoke to had had the first baby of the New Year fifteen years ago, and Maggie Bielby had visited the maternity ward in the small hours of the morning. She still has the reporter's picture, framed on her wall."

"Bielby was always plugging the decline of decent domesticity in the *Examiner*. People took their cue from that, and the Bielbys were identified with happy family life. But under the surface, folk don't really believe it. At least, they believe it about Maggie; they only *say* it about Bielby."

"Anything more concrete than that?"

"I heard it said half a dozen times that they'd nothing against Bielby; then they'd go on to say that Maggie had deserved someone better."

"And no reasons given?"

"They just didn't seem to trust Bielby."

"Yet they voted for him in elections! Did any of you come across any clear hint that ties Bielby up with the Shopping Centre fiasco?"

"Everyone seems to take that for granted. One man told me that Bielby deserved a knighthood for all he'd

got moving in the High Street—browbeating trades-
men to fork out for the Civic Trust project—but that
on the Town Moor he had bitten off more than he
could chew."

"Full stop?"

"He went on chuntering about the Forty Thieves,
but as soon as you ask who they are, heads are sadly
shaken."

"Does the man in the street connect Bielby with
Mawdesley?"

"Oddly enough, Mawdesley seems well liked. Yet
nobody was surprised that he got his in the end. And
nobody tries to defend him. But as one shopkeeper
put it, if everybody who pinched half a million spread
it around as Mawdesley did, there'd be more towns in
the country as much worth living in as Filton."

"But do they associate Bielby with Mawdesley's
fiddles?"

"I'm sure they do—but they won't come out and
say so. God: what sort of evidence is this?"

"In the present exercise, first rate. Do go on,
Sergeant."

"I think the general feeling is that there, but for the
grace of God, went Bielby, too. But no one will say
why, because I don't think that anyone knows. In fact
a gentlemen's outfitter on the corner of Peel Street and
Union Lane went so far as to say that Bielby ought to
have gone down instead of Mawdesley. I had to buy
a bow tie to get that out of him. I hope that will be all
right on expenses?"

Kenworthy ignored the point.

"The odd thing is that my gentlemen's outfitter didn't

seem to understand the ins and outs of Mawdesley's
frauds."

"And do you, Sergeant Cooper?"

"Roughly, sir."

"Good. I have to summarize them for my interim
report. You can draft a paragraph for me."

Then Sergeant Widgeon introduced a new line of
thought.

"There is something that might be important, sir."

"Go on."

"Well, it's like the things Bill Cooper's been
talking about: something you can't pin down."

"For God's sake, Widgeon, haven't you got it into
your head yet that today's operations was precisely a
quest for things that can't be pinned down? Let's hold
them up to the light and look at them. We can pin
them down later."

"Well, I picked up a hint more than once, a
suggestion—particularly strong among people who'd
been rehoused after the demolition of the Town
Moor—that somewhere in Maggie's past there'd been
a big, dark, secret love. Oh, nothing insidious;
nothing, of course, actually immoral, this being
Filton-in-Leckerfield. People were anxious to stress
that. They were on Maggie's side all down the line."

"Who?" Kenworthy asked, the fraying of his
patience showing through.

"You'll never believe this: Herbert Tunnicliffe."

"Good grief!" Inspector Heald said. "He must be
thirty years older than her."

"Nineteen, to be exact," Kenworthy muttered.

"The thing is that out on the Town Moor the
Tunnicliffes had the maintenance contract, for what

that was worth, on all the slum property. Not much work ever got done, because the Mawdesleys—the present Mawdesley's father, in those days—were too tightfisted. But there's no doubt that the Leyland house got special favours. Herbert Tunnicliffe was in 12 Elgin Row more often than in any other house on the estate. And that continued throughout the Second World War—after Maggie's stepfather had died and her mother had become bedridden."

Cooper entered the discussion again.

"It's a funny thing. This was so vague that I wasn't going to mention it—but I came across the same story in a couple of places. Well, not so much a story as an insinuation; only it wasn't Herbert Tunnicliffe who was mentioned. It was his brother William. The tale was the same as Mike Widgeon's—only someone's mixed up. It was *after* the Bielbys were married. They had to go on living in Elgin Row for a few months, and there were running repairs that Bielby was paying for out of his own pocket to keep the place barely habitable. But it was William not Herbert, who was always calling—when Bielby was out. William, of course, can't be more than five or six years older than Maggie."

."Four," Kenworthy said. "The baby of the family."

And he went over and unhooked the wedding group from the wall, took it back to his chair. The resemblance between Maggie and her mother in their dove-grey costumes was a tribute to Bielby's power of description; but then, he had probably relied on this picture, rather than memory. In the back row there was a hatchet-faced Amazon with her arms folded across her chest. At her side stood a tall craggy man with clipped but tousled locks falling over his forehead like a bullock's. At one end of the front row stood Sid Wheeler, at the beginning of his gangling years. The picture had been taken a couple of hours before the policeman had called on the errand that led him to the birching-stool; barely half an hour before he had started his first crude courtship of Maggie with a disgusting glass bubble stuck up one nostril.

An awkward silence, a mixture of credulity and impatience, even the beginnings of dissipation of whatever confidence they had in their chief, fell over the conference as Kenworthy sat and paid more attention to the picture than he did to his colleagues. Then he jerked himself back into consciousness, like a man awakened by an alarm clock. He passed the picture on for the others to see. They took it in turn, glanced at it with polite interest. Then Inspector Heald could stand his own inactivity no longer.

"Far be it from me to suggest that anything I've done today could match the brilliance and urgency of what we've been listening to—"

"Yes, do please tell us, Inspector."

"I've spent much of my day thinking. There's room for that too, I presume, in such cases as this?"

He picked up his clipboard, which was leaning against the leg of his chair.

"A preliminary point: how far ought we to be trusting our local colleagues? It seems to me, with a man like Bielby calling the tune in this Borough—"

"Don't think I haven't worried on that score," Kenworthy said mildly. "But I feel easy in mind about it now—since a few minutes ago, when I was given unwitting information about a bag of golf clubs."

Abashed by his casual tone, Heald slashed an angry tick against one of the items on his sheet.

"Then there's the question of weapons. Are we paying enough attention to them? Who knew that Bielby had an illicit 7.65? Who knew where he kept it? I have taken the liberty of visiting this so-called Crown and Cushion Club, and I've talked to the Steward. And it's fairly clear that every man in that Club—which means virtually anyone who is anyone in the town—must have known. Bielby was a braggart. He had had the thing since the war. When there was an outbreak of burglaries a year or two ago, he told his friends openly that he kept it loaded in a drawer of his bedside cabinet; boasted that he wouldn't be afraid to use it."

Heald paused to assess the effect of his point. Kenworthy nodded appreciation.

"Not perhaps very far-reaching; but a tangible fact. Now consider the other gun. We know from the calibre that it was a Luger. We presume from the accuracy of the firing, that it was fitted to fire from the shoulder. Given that and the range, the shooting required no great expertise. Any man with infantry musket-training, even perhaps only in the Home Guard, might have pulled it off. But this gives us something else vital to go on. We know that these things were brought back as souvenirs from the war, and some were not handed in despite periods of grace. Who, locally, might have brought one back? Or bought it? Or know from whom he could buy it? These might be fruitful questions. The firearm has never been found, though Gibson's squad spent days looking. We ought to start looking again."

He lifted the first sheet from his clip, and it could be seen that he had done another of his charts, with a long list of names and ruled columns for eliminating crosses.

"We now come to something more exclusive. We know that Mrs. Bielby was in bed when she was shot. The point has been made that she might have been asleep at the time. But would she have been, so few minutes after she had rung her husband at Mrs. Fielding's? Is it not more likely that she was in bed when she rang? There is an extension up there. But why should she have done that, unless there was someone with her, prompting, perhaps threatening? That possibility has been mooted; but have we followed it up? Must it not have been someone—again, the possibility has been referred to—to whose presence in her bedroom she did not object? Of course, we may be wrong about that. He may have got in by violence or threat. And this secret lover of old; ought we not to be following him up, and not just chatting amicably to people on corners about him?"

"If we hadn't chatted to people on corners," Kenworthy said, "we might never have heard of him."

"And finally—"

Heald laid the board on his knee.

"I really think we ought to get down in proper detail to the nature of these fraudulent practices."

Kenworthy answered amiably.

"It would take each and any of us several days, at a rough guess, really to master the evidence given at the Mawdesley trial: even from the books simplified for presentation to a jury. I shall be referring some aspects of this case to our own Fraud Squad. But such things have been known to take a staff of two hundred officers and professional accountants as long as two years—to produce a negative result. I'd prefer to make an arrest this week."

But he had set up another train of thought in the Inspector's mind.

"Bielby's son is an accountant, isn't he? It wouldn't have created any stir if he had walked into his mother's room."

"Inspector Heald, tomorrow you may take yourself off, with my full authority, and tackle this case from any angle that appeals to you. You may have both sergeants. You may ask Superintendent Bartram for any assistance he can spare you; and my guess is that he would be lavish with it. I am sure that Inspector Gibson would happily drop most other things to put himself and his team at your disposal. And I promise you that I myself will move into action along any fruitful lines that you can unearth. But—"

Kenworthy looked down again, almost affectionately, at the photograph.

"But first I want about an hour each with two people who grace this happy family group. That is, if they're still alive."

The conference broke up a few minutes after that, but within an hour Kenworthy had been called out of bed.

It was Inspector Gibson, ringing his room from reception. The Filton inspector had spent the day and evening doggedly trying to trace anyone who might have seen an intruder leaving the rear of the Bielbys' premises on the night of the first murder. Less than two hours ago, one of his men had seen a couple approach a grassy love-nest that he had been watching, a well-frequented hollow in a rough patch of ground behind *Notre Repos*. Kenworthy had Gibson come up at once; received him in his disreputable pyjamas.

There were red spots of passionate enthusiasm burning over Gibson's cheek-bones. He had been working furiously all day, and it looked as if it had paid off. It was the usual story; a hangdog couple who had not come forward with information because they dared not reveal their presence together in that place. Gibson was in no mood for patient psychological interrogation. He got the facts out of those two as much by sheer willpower as by threats and tactics.

The pair had been in the habit of approaching their Eden by way of Sandringham Avenue and along an overgrown right of way that ran between houses and gardens. They had seen no man come away from the Bielbys'—they were too deeply engrossed in their own affairs. But on the night that mattered, on their way out there, they had seen a car parked outside *Notre Repos*. A vintage car, in exemplary trim. The young man was something of an automobile buff, and he knew an Alvis straight-eight front-wheel-drive when he saw one.

An Alvis—

Mawdesley had collected Alvis cars; but Gibson gave Kenworthy no time to leap to the connection. The whole of Mawdesley's museum-piece collection had come under the hammer in the general liquidation of his assets. But Gibson knew what had happened to them. Bielby had bought one of them—and made it over to his brother-in-law.

Cliff—

"Locate him," Kenworthy said.

"Already done. You were talking about him yesterday to Superintendent Bartram, so we already had feelers out. He's in Yorkshire. No record; no form since that first Borstal sentence. A trained mechanic; but it isn't for craftsmanship that he's made his name. He's a wildcat troublemaker as to the manner born."

And Gibson mentioned the name of a factory that had not had an uninterrupted month's work for three years.

"One just wonders," Gibson said, "whether he had any hand in coordinating the sabotage on the Town Moor, while the Tunnicliffes were struggling."

Gibson was still burning for the chase.

"And one wonders too," Kenworthy ruminated, "whether he might not have been able to walk into his half-sister's bedroom without too much fuss being made. I mean, I don't think she'd be overjoyed at the sight of him. But she wouldn't start a hue and cry until she'd heard what he wanted, would she?"

·12·

KENWORTHY MANOEUVRED HEALD and himself to a
table for two at breakfast time—in spite of an elderly
morning waitress for whom any change of habit was
a threat of anarchy. Inspector Heald, brought up-to-
date on events, naturally assumed that Kenworthy
would take over the interrogation of Cliff.

"The night Bielby was arrested," Kenworthy said,
"even Gibson's own County DS, Hallam, was content
to leave the donkey work to him. It was something I
went into in some detail, because I wanted to know
whether there'd been any attempt in high places to get
Bielby off the hook. I'm giving Gibson his head.
He'll deliver the goods—if there are any to be
delivered. How are you spending your day? Over
accounts?"

Heald smiled wanly. The acrimony of last evening's conference was spent, leaving in its place a gap
which he saw no way of bridging.

"No. Of course, you were right about that side of
things."

"A new hunt for the Luger, then?"

"I doubt if we can improve on what was done before we got here."

The cold light of morning—

"Spend the day with me, then."

Kenworthy knew where they were going, led them to a complex of 1960-ish housing on a plateau on the southeastern edge of town. At its heart was a hollow square of old folks' bungalows, set round austere lawns and fiercely pruned rose beds.

"Young people are funny," Kenworthy said. "Bielby thought Martha Garbutt was as old as the hills. She can't have been past her late forties when he was a boy."

But she was old now. The little two-roomed dwelling, overheated in spite of the warmth of the day, smelled sourly of age: of incontinence, flaking skin and an incarcerated cat.

"We do encourage them to have their own things around them—hoping, of course, that they won't want to bring too much."

That was the warden, apologizing for the incongruity of the Garbutt treasures against the clinical efficiency of the design (a Bielby conception, architect Hopwood, conveyancing by Hibbert, rake-offs according to previous pattern?). Martha Garbutt had reconstituted her corner of Swallow Street: a monumental and monumentally depressing cabinet of pinned moths, arranged in concentric circles, their pigment sun-bleached, their wings dry and disintegrating. She was a huge woman, grotesquely starch-fed and under-exercised. It was difficult to imagine what shape her body bore beneath her sweat-ridden layers of subfusc clothing.

Kenworthy quite properly introduced them as police officers, whereupon she retreated behind dementia that may or may not have been genuine. ("Like all these old dears, she is sometimes a little confused," the warden had said.) She distrusted the police, had reason, one guessed, to remember past fears, through the disorientated layers of her time-sense. Her contributions to the tidal surges of the Playground had not been limited to midwifery and laying-out. She had not been beyond a back bedroom abortion; if she strictly approved of the case.

"She came here to pay me ten shillings she owed."

Kenworthy waited and hoped that the vapours might clear.

"It's Maggie Leyland we wanted to talk to you about."

"She never came to me. I never even brought her into the world. Her mother had the *doctor*."

Spoken as if that was treachery to the ethics of the Town Moor.

"And who paid for that?"

"Ask those who know."

The overheating was oppressive. Heald felt the sweat straining out of his forehead. Martha Garbutt's scrambled brain clung to the catch-words of a life-time, evoked by the familiar theme.

"She should never have married him. I told her so at the time."

On the wall was a framed Schools Inspector's Certificate, awarded to her mother in the 1880s.

"The night her mother died—he had taken her out to dinner and fallen out with the waiter. That ought to have shown her what he was like, if nothing else did. She let herself in for a cat-and-dog life."

Outside, an old woman was talking loudly to a vocationally ebullient young milkman.

"What did they quarrel about?" Kenworthy asked.

"About a piece of bread."

"No. I mean Sid Wheeler and Maggie Leyland."

"About that swine's old grandmother, for one thing. Because he would never go to see her—and Maggie refused not to pass the time of day with her. Then they fell out, were forever falling out, over Cliff."

She became embroiled in a bronchial wheeze, and had difficulty retrieving a handkerchief on which she was half-sitting.

"I told her to get on without Cliff. He was no good to either of them. It was a mercy to the pair of them when they did put him inside. But her mother had made her promise, only a day or two before she died, that she would always look after her brother. You couldn't shake Maggie about anything like that."

Her marble and bronze clock, flanked by marble and bronze Grecian urns, had a bronchial attack of its own, prior to striking the half-hour.

"Is it your palm you want read? Or shall I get the cards out?"

Oddly, it was only Kenworthy she asked. She totally ignored Heald the whole time he was in the house.

"I always think you get better truth out of the cards though, of course, I have to charge more."

"How much?" Kenworthy asked.

"Five shillings. Twenty-five, in new pence."

So Kenworthy let her drag herself to her feet, and she lumbered about the room and spread her cards on the frayed damask tablecloth. And Heald thought that Kenworthy was at least going to ask her if the cards knew who had killed Maggie Leyland. But all she talked was a farrago of dark stranger, unexpected visitor conventions; and she talked it as if she believed it, and expected Kenworthy to believe it as well. And when she looked up from her concentration on the queen of spades, her grasp of events had vanished again, and she had forgotten who her own unexpected visitors were.

"Have you come about the tally club? You'll find the money in the biscuit barrel."

"I'm sorry," Kenworthy said, as he led Heald alongside rose beds to the other side of the close. "I didn't think she'd be so far gone. We might fare even worse at our next call. Still—it's worth a throw."

And if Bielby in his youth had thought that Martha Garbutt was old, he must surely be excused for having made any mistake about this next character. The man who came to the door was in his nineties: spare, with thin skin like papyrus, flecked with brown spots; but recognizable—still with a tuft of independent hair trying to curl down over his forehead.

"Mr. Randall?"

"Come in, gentlemen. Ah can guess who you are, though Ah don't know what use I can be to you."

"You must excuse me," Kenworthy said, "if I yield to temptation and just call you Top-Notch. I think perhaps you'd prefer that?"

And the former tram driver grinned, stooping as he led them into his home, delighted at the reminder of

his reputation. Largely apocryphal, that, no doubt—
the man who had always driven with his power lever
hard over; but at least he had made his gesture to the
age in which he was being compelled to live. He was
well-preserved—brittle, with the fragility of a physical frame wearing away, but a disciplined man, who
had always respected his limitations, and lived without excesses of any kind. He spoke in a fruity dialect
that was itself a throwback to another epoch—when
men had mattered more than uniformity. And his
room was full of bookcases, newspapers, albums and
cuttings.

"We came to see you," Kenworthy said, "because
I should think you knew Roger Bielby-Sid Wheeler
better than anyone else in Filton."

"Nay, that's pitching it a bit strong, man."

"Did you know—no, there's no way you could
know—that he wrote a memoir while he was held on
remand? And among the stories he told was how he
met you one day on the Blackpool Front, and told
you—before he knew it himself—that his mother was
going to marry Arthur Bielby. Between the lines, you
know, Top-Notch, he appreciated you."

"Ah remember that day. Ah'm glad he remembered
it."

"You must be one of the few people in this town
who actually liked the lad."

And Randall put the tips of his fingers together and
paused a trifle weightily before replying—in the
manner that Bielby himself had described.

"Ah've been taught to look for that of God in every
man."

He could use a religious phrase as unconcernedly as he could look at the clock on his mantelpiece.

"He should never have come back to Filton, but he was under a compulsion. St. Paul, when he'd seen what he'd seen on the road to Damascus, heard the voice in his heart and asked 'Lord, what wouldst thou have me do?' Ah don't think that Roger Bielby ever heard a voice after that fashion. But Ah met him one day on the Playground, not long after he'd settled here, and we'd a long talk together. He was coming back south, you know, from a flying job he'd been trying to do up in Scotland. And he got off the train at Preston. And he didn't know why. And he didn't know why he wandered along to the platform where the Filton train was waiting. And he didn't know why he got on it. But he came back to Filton, and he never could get away again. And he saw Maggie Leyland, and he couldn't get away from her again, ever."

Randall made several unsuccessful attempts to pinch a stray thread from the knee of his trousers.

"Filton was bad in those days. They were bad old days. There was one poor old man called Isaac Mosley who killed himself. And Roger had come along just as he was going to do it. And he told the lad he was going to do it—because he wanted the lad out of the way. But Roger went and fetched him his razor. I told you—they were terrible days. He just wanted something big to happen. Then, in the war, he dropped a bomb on a place in a panic and things got mixed up in his head, and it was as if it was the Town Moor he'd blown up. He'd destroyed *a* Town Moor. And he came back here. And he did big things for this town."

"He did other things too," Kenworthy said.

"Judge not, that ye be not judged. He was like any other of us. He was a mixture of men."

"He had to make his own living, as well as what he did for Filton. What's known as feathering one's nest."

"Ah've no doubt that he thought he was doing his best by his family."

"Who was his sponsor?" Kenworthy asked. "Who helped him over the chasm, so that he could carry out his reforms of Filton from a position of comfort? Whose power—and that means money—was he wielding?"

There followed another of Randall's silences.

"Nay," he said. "Tha'll not trip me into saying owt as Ah can't prove."

"Top-Notch, I'm not trying to trip you into anything. Was it Mawdesley?"

Randall noticed that Kenworthy's hand went to his pocket, then came away empty.

"Light thy pipe, man, if it'll make thee more comfy."

Kenworthy rubbed brown flake in the palm of his hand, stuffed the bowl of his pipe, lit it and produced a curl of blue smoke.

"When Roger Bielby came back to Filton," Randall said. "He thought he knew the ways of the world. He'd been to South Africa. He'd been a fighting officer and learned the way of life of an élite. And he came back here and couldn't even get proper respect from a waiter in a restaurant. And he and Francis Mawdesley were daggers-drawn in the early days. Roger didn't want the demolition of the Town Moor.

He wanted something done about the property as it stood. He didn't want everybody transferred lock, stock and barrel to a tower up Coldsprings. But of course that ran counter to Francis Mawdesley's plans; and old Jethro Burgess was giving him a pretty free hand in the *Examiner*. Then suddenly Roger and Francis Mawdesley were friends. Francis Mawdesley was an astute man; he could see what there was in Roger. He got him to go with him for a drink, after a protest meeting they'd had about the Playground. After that, they were firm friends—and Roger's affairs began to look up. Till then, he hadn't even been able to escape from Elgin Row. There was an appalling shortage of houses, and he couldn't raise the deposit on a new one."

"You mean Mawdesley bought Bielby, the way he might have bought himself a new shopping precinct— or a new wing for a church school?"

"I don't know anything, Mr. Kenworthy, except the course of events."

"But you know who killed Maggie and Roger Bielby?"

"I do not know."

"But you know what you think."

"I know what I think. And there's nowt so dangerous as what a man only thinks."

It was plain that there was no force in the hands of man that could make Randall voice a mere supposition.

"But there's one question I know you can answer for me—that you won't want to answer—and won't refuse to, either—because if I'm right about your beliefs, there is something about absolute truth."

And Randall looked at Kenworthy with uneasy expectancy—not untinged with shrewd admiration for his tactics.

"Ah s'll have to hear t' question, first."

"Who was Maggie Leyland's father?"

The old man told them. And Heald was aware of something almost seraphic in the relief that came over Kenworthy's features.

"Thank you, Top-Notch."

· 13 ·

GIBSON WAS STILL away, gone to fetch Cliff to help
with enquiries, when Kenworthy and Heald returned
to the station. Bielby Junior had called to collect his
bag of clubs, against signature. Bartrum was in an
irrepressibly jovial mood.

"Want to come to a party?"

"The only party I'm looking forward to is a quiet,
highly exclusive one after certain voluntary state-
ments have been signed and found to support each
other."

"Aye, well, that'll come. I was thinking of the
Crown and Cushion Club. It's Founders' Night tonight. You can come as my guest. Your whole outfit
can come as my guests."

"I'm not sure yet how my outfit's going to be
occupied this evening."

Gibson brought Cliff in at about eleven-thirty.
Kenworthy was still minded to leave him to it, but he
made sure he had a good look at Maggie's half-
brother whilst he was being documented: a burly man
in his late forties, deliberately badly kempt to convey
the right spirit of aggression; an appearance calculated

to offend those whom he wanted to offend—which meant society's quiet, respectable types. He was the sort of man who could make defiers of a picket line feel that they had been done violence, though none had been offered; the sort who was resented by his union bosses as much as by local management; the sort of man who after a trouncing, after a settlement had been agreed in spite of all he had fought for, was still the unchallenged leader of those who had weakened.

At half past one, Gibson had sandwiches sent into the interview room. At two he came out to the urinal, shook his head at Kenworthy in frustration. At five he came out and took Kenworthy aside.

"Still can't shake him. He was at the Bielbys' that night, had been there previous nights. But he didn't kill Maggie and doesn't know who did. What is more, he has an alibi for the morning Bielby was killed, which I'm having checked out in Yorkshire, and which I have a horrible feeling is going to hold."

"That could fit. Don't hog-tie yourself by believing that one man did both killings. And go on scaring him."

"Oh, he's scared. He's got no idea that he might be getting fair play or a square deal off me. Any minute now he's going to offer to blow the gaff on the Forty Thieves, if only I'll listen to sense about the murders."

"Well, do a deal, then. I'll be quite happy to step in later and refuse to keep your side of the bargain. This isn't Lord Cricket Ground."

At five-thirty, Kenworthy showed another sign of life. He went along to see Bartram.

"I think I'd like to come to your Crown and Cushion after all. I think all my lads would, too. And it would do Brother Gibson a power of good to leave Cliff for an hour or two, thinking things out."

"Easily arranged. I can tell you, it's going to be quite a night."

"It will be, if a little idea of mine comes off. The only thing is, I'd like to bring a guest of my own."

"Bring the Man in the Moon if you like. I'll answer to the committee for him."

Kenworthy disappeared from the station.

· 14 ·

THE CROWN AND Cushion was a green enclave in the redbrick road that had once been the desirable residences of Filton's cotton masters. Even now, the club might have gone unheeded by the uninitiated, not a stone's throw behind the new-look High Street, and only a house or two away from Mawdesley's. The Crown of the name was one of the most meticulously founded, certainly one of the most lovingly tended bowling-greens in northen England. A cool lawn in the shade of tall chestnuts and a twelve-foot mellowed wall, it was overlooked by a spectators' verandah outside the billiard room (equipped by Mawdesley) the card rooms, the smoking room and the bar (2p off town pub prices).

Few men who amounted to anything in Filton were not members, even though some of them did not come often. There were some who came every night, some who put in a predictable weekly appearance: but it was not done to miss Founders' Night. There was an atmosphere in the Crown and Cushion suggestive of a haven where discretion could be taken for granted; and perhaps that was one of the most dangerous

illusions in the town. But even for Coronations,
Jubilees and Victory Days, the members did not
indulge in the debilitating luxury of a Ladies' Night.

At a quarter past six Kenworthy had looked into the
interview room to see how things fared between
Gibson and Cliff. The completed sheets of the statement in progress lay askew on the table, as yet
uninitialled. Kenworthy fingered them casually towards himself, read them without revealing a reaction. Cliff looked round at him with resigned distaste
for his sort.

"Is he being a good boy, Inspector?"

"His memory is improving from minute to
minute," Gibson said.

In fact Cliff, wheeling and dealing in quantities
trickily unknown to him, was being neurotically
careful what he said—and had already unveiled a
hundred per cent more than he had intended as Gibson
ironed out minor inconsistencies, ensnaring him
deeper in every other sentence. Gibson knew how it
was done.

It had been when a prison sentence for Mawdesley
had begun to appear inevitable that Bielby—very
likely with Mawdesley's consent—had reversed the
policy of three decades and let the Tunnicliffes in on
the Town Moor project. Cliff had not yet got round to
filling in the detail of his own role in the easing out of
the local builders. There were some aspects of it—
including grievous bodily harm to a clerk of works—
that Gibson was craftily allowing to be glossed over
for the time being.

They had progressed to the time when the Tunnicliffes were phased out, and Mawdesley was adjust-

ing himself to the routine of slopping out, and trying
to acquire for his balsa aircraft modelling the brand of
intoxicating adhesive which he could peddle for snout
to the barons who sniffed it for kicks. It was now that
Bielby started thinking—and talking—in terms of the
just steward. Mawdesley had shunted funds away in
his wife's name, and when she divorced him she had
achieved a greater degree of double-crossing than he
himself had managed in a lifetime. There was not a lot
left, but there was a credit balance for a remote
holding company created some years ago for opportunist ventures. It operated on two out of three
signatures, one of which was Bielby's. And this had
brought Gibson to the now unavoidable question: who
were the Forty Thieves? Cliff could not avoid the
answer now: Bielby, Hopwood, Hibbert and two
others who had not come into the story so far, and
whose names would not become public property until
the Fraud Squad and the DPP had worked through
their patient processes. This was a bonus, but beside
the main point. What mattered crucially was that
Bielby, bent now on self-glorification as much as on
personal gain, suddenly determined that there was to
be not merely one nest-egg, but a whole clutch of
them waiting for Mawdesley when he eventually
came out. The first move was to cash in on the next
phase of the Town Moor development, the founda-
tions for which had already been laid before Mawdesley was shunted into the sidings. Cliff mentioned a
firm of contractors whose name would be nationally
explosive. Comprehensive details had been settled,
including heavily discounted transactions for builder's
merchandise, the substitution of materials cheaper

than specification, the waiving of obstructive building standards, and premiums for the preferential allocation of leases. Then the worst had happened: the firm concerned had suddenly got cold feet, presumably when the full impact of the Mawdesley connection had sunk in in the boardroom. They simply did not put in a tender. And at this stage a majority vote of the Forty Thieves was in favour of quiescence. Hibbert had been particularly anxious to avoid further involvement. But Bielby, signing, with one of the partners still an unknown, had command of the funds.

And how did Cliff know all this?

For most of his life, he had had little to do with Filton or Bielby. He had come out of Borstal knowing several things, not the least graphic of which had been that he had had enough of such places. As the saying went, he had gone straight; though there had lingered from his old ideas a deep-rooted dissatisfaction with the unequal roles that he and the establishment were playing in the ordering of his existence. On an assembly line his true worth went unappreciated, and from there to legitimate—or at least, not illegal—subversion had been an easy step. Organized protest, with withdrawal of labour at any time, on any issue, at the drop of anyone's hat, had become the way of his life. Cliff had found, at first to his surprise, that men had listened to him. And Bielby, who knew of his renown from the grapevine, had not been slow to conscript him when he needed him.

"It was only aggro, you know. And if you'd seen, as I did, the use the Tunnicliffes made of their workforce, you'd see nothing to be ashamed of in that."

No; he himself had never worked on the Town Moor site. Well, just once or twice he had slipped over for a word with the site convenors. Just to give them a tip or two about organizing themselves—all according to the accepted laws and usages of industrial warfare. Cliff said nothing about bodily harm to the watchdogs of the establishment; and clearly it had suited Gibson's strategy to give such things a very low profile indeed—at this juncture. And no; Bielby had not paid him any kind of fee for this work. It was hardly work, was it, standing up for the rights of honest labour against the exploiting classes? But there had been out-of-pocket expenses: time off from his own work; nights away from home; entertainment of committees. And when it came to settling for these, Bielby had started dragging his feet.

Because Bielby, you see, had over-extended himself over this Town Moor affair. He had gone on to think things out for himself. That was the trouble with Bielby. He never had realized that he was nothing more than a weapon in other men's hands. What they could do, he could do. He had bought himself in through the perimeters of another contractor: against Hibbert's advice, against Hopwood's advice, against the will of Mawdesley, visited in gaol. Just sit tight and quiet until Mawdesley was out and about again, that was the ticket. But Bielby, the clever bugger, wanted to show what a clever bugger he was. He went it alone—on the rest of Mawdesley's money; new palms to be crossed, new introductions to key figures to be bought; Mediterranean holidays to be laid on for those who still needed persuading, men with vital votes at the boardroom table to be sweetened. Until, one fine morning, Bielby discovered that he had been dealing with cleverer buggers than himself. For the second time, an expected tender did not come in; and there is no remedy at law for the misapplication of corrupt payments.

There wasn't even enough left in the kitty to reimburse Cliff for eight journeys from Leeds to Filton and back; which speaks for itself as to how much remained to Mawdesley's sinking fund.

Yes, well, Cliff had come back two or three times to see what he could get out of the ruins. Life was bloody expensive, and he'd had twenty-three weeks on social security in the last year. Yes; he'd been to *Notre Repos* three or four times in the weeks before Maggie's death. (Gibson was suggestively vague about how many times the Alvis had been spotted.)

Only that bugger Bielby had not been in when he called. He didn't know where he was. Maggie didn't know where he was. Of course, he knew now that Bielby had been out laying some bloody Catholic.

How did he find that out? Well, you couldn't get blood out of a stone, and you couldn't squeeze sweat out of Maggie. So this last time, he hadn't gone straight to her house. He had been to see Mawdesley, to see what he was doing about what was owing to him. Mawdesley had told him what company Bielby was keeping. And together they had gone to *Notre Repos*, to wait the night out, if necessary.

There is a unique quality that marks any piece of continuous prose that has been produced in the first instance as the answers to a series of loaded questions.

* * *

My sister was always a soft bitch, and when we were kids she was bossy. I have seen very little of her over the last twenty years. But you can't tell me that she was married all that time to that bloody shyster without having some idea of what was going on. I mean, it stands to sense, doesn't it, that he wasn't earning that kind of money writing up cat shows for that bloody rag he was on? I reckon her conscience was always a matter of not knowing what she didn't want to know.

When we got there that night, Mawdesley was in no mood for wrapping this up. He told her that Bielby had made a pig's ear of the Town Moor, that he owed us both money, and he wasn't stirring away from here tonight until Bielby had come home and he'd called him to account for it. Then she started coming the innocent simpleton, which riled Mawdesley. And he went round the house pointing to things. And he asked her where she thought this and that had come from, the stereogram and the etchings on the wall, and her tumbler-drier. And she got up-tight about that, and said it was hard-earned money. And when he heard that, Mawdesley started laughing like a closet. I have never heard anything like it. I thought he was going off his crust. And then she began to cotton on, and she wanted to know if it was because of us that the Tunnicliffes had gone out of business. And she said that if she thought there'd been that kind of monkey-business, she'd go to the police about it, first thing in the morning, even if it meant shopping her own husband. Because she was sick to death of it all.

And she was going to bed now, and would we please leave.

Well, we did leave, because we weren't getting anywhere, and not likely to. And you can ask Mawdesley about that, because I ran him down to his place in my car. And as for the other time, the morning Bielby got what was coming to him, I was with a coach party, going to do picket duty outside a film processing place down south. You can ask anyone who was on it.

Kenworthy beckoned Gibson out into the corridor.

"Watch the time. You can keep him on ice for a bit. The Founders' Dinner is half past seven for eight."

Gibson made a wry face. He found the Crown and Cushion no sort of counter-attraction to the prospect of getting Cliff finally tied up.

"I shall want you there," Kenworthy said. "I'm hoping I'll need you."

There was not much elbow room—there was a full house at the Crown and Cushion. A good meal was served by outside caterers, the hired waitresses the only females on the premises, and they causing a somewhat pathetic stir among the middle-aged men, being out-of-town girls and mostly personable.

The town elders were all there: Superintendent Bartram, who, unlike Gibson, would not have missed a Founders' Night for any consideration; the Tunnicliffes, Herbert in a dress suit of a cut that had been fashionable in the 1930s, little William with already enough beer under his belt to have reached the prattling and giggling stage; Fielding, with his sparse frame and dirty grey

hair, quiet and unsmiling, and not exactly surrounded by
a pack of friends, but clearly not off his food; Jeremy
Hibbert, nodding to Kenworthy as if they were associ-
ates from distant days; and a variety of high-class
tobacconists, seed-salesmen, iron-mongers, not forgetting their accountants and bank-managers. The force
was well represented, too, and so equably spread among
the crowd that more than one diner remarked that it
looked as if they were planted ready for trouble: Cooper
and Widgeon talking to men they had got to know
during their earlier enquiries; Heald with the Borough
Librarian; Gibson in the middle of a group whom
Kenworthy did not know.

But the greatest stir so far had been created by the
man whom Kenworthy had brought in as his "guest."
They had come in fairly late in the pre-drinks half-
hour, and the bar had already been so crowded that a
number had escaped through the large doors that
stood open on to the bowling green. And into this
gathering, Kenworthy politely ushered Mawdesley, at
the sight of whom there was a sudden hush in the
immediate vicinity. Rapidly and infectiously it spread
round the whole assembly, so that even those outside
turned their heads to try to see what had occasioned it.
Then someone, perhaps braver than most, or maybe
more attached to good form, nodded to the mill-owner
and some sort of fissure made crow's feet across the
ice. Bartram came across from the counter with drinks
and treated Mawdesley as if they were everyday pals.
Someone else clasped his elbow and made incoherent
but recognizably welcoming noises. By the end of the
meal, one would have thought him the most popular
man in the club.

After the meal, a tradition: Brown Ball. Men had been looking forward to it with a sort of puerile eagerness. They were agog for it. Several had asked Kenworthy whether he would be playing.

The Crown and Cushion Club were civilized diners: there were no after-dinner speeches. As soon as coffee had been served, a number of enthusiasts went out to the green to play a few ends in the lingering late spring twilight. But the majority edged towards the billiard room to play or to see, the more prudent of them taking up positions from which they had a field of vision without being actually in the room.

Brown Ball: it was alleged to be a Royal Naval invention: someone even claimed to tell Kenworthy the name of the ship in whose ward-room it had originated. The first phase of the game was for all the players—and that meant any man who volunteered for the sport—to make a rush at the tables and stuff his pockets with billiard and snooker balls, the entire stock of which had been laid out for the rush. Only one brown was left lying on one of the tables, and this was the target.

It was a game for the bloods. The players ranged themselves about the walls of the room, and when the year's president called a man's name, that man had to take a ball from his pocket and hurl it across the room at the brown ball. If he missed, it cost him a round of drinks for all other players. Simple and joyous. The hilarity—and general peril—depended on the speed with which names were called: and the reigning president thoroughly understood the spirit of the game. Sergeant Widgeon was the only policeman to risk his dignity. William Tunnicliffe, not exactly drunk, but boyishly happy, was surely the keenest and least accurate of the players. His brother took no part in the game, and was among the more timorous of the spectators, watching from outside the room, at several angles removed from the danger of a ricochet, a thin smile on his face, as if he had a sort of benign pity for the foibles of mankind. Kenworthy watched for a few minutes, then began a slow, systematic promenade round the crowd, speaking first to Cooper, then Heald, then Bartram, then finally Gibson.

"How far did you get with him, Inspector?"

"Not much further than I was when you left us."

He still resented having been taken away from his quarry.

"It's frustrating," Kenworthy said, "when you *know*. And you know too that you aren't going to find any proof. Our only hope's a confession; which means pressure on nerves."

"You mean Cliff's nerves?"

"No. Cliff didn't do it. He may have been an accessory, but I'm not sure whether he was a conscious one. I'm going to conduct this in public, to add to the tension. I've asked Bartram to get the steward to clear one of the smaller card rooms, and he's going to shepherd a few people in there at about half past ten. In the meanwhile, I want you to go back to the station. See what keys Cliff has on him, and see if one of them is to the front door of *Notre Repos*. If he has one, then my case probably collapses. Oh, and make sure that he knows what you're up to. Watch his reaction."

And that was the moment at which a commotion in the billiard room suggested an accident: not, surely, for the first time in the history of Brown Ball. There was a loose scrum, which had to be called on to make way for an injured man. William Tunnicliffe: and the first impression from a distance was that he was very seriously injured indeed. It took some time to revive him.

"It's time the committee stopped this blood stupid game."

"It cost the club thirty quid for broken fittings last year."

"How the hell did you get Mawdesley here?" Gibson asked.

"He was reluctant—and I'm afraid I had to become a trifle authoritarian. Three and a half years of gaol seem to have got him into compliant habits."

There was no doctor in the house, but there was a male nurse, who keenly wanted William Tunnicliffe taken to hospital. But the active little man, once he had been brought round, would hear nothing of the kind. The ball in full flight had caught him on the cheekbone, mercifully missing his eye, though the contusion was going to give him what everyone promised would be a real beauty. He insisted that his vision had not been affected and that he only wanted to sit quietly in a corner for a while. Someone brought him a neat double whisky. Kenworthy continued his wanderings round the club. Men came up and spoke to him, just for the sake of doing so. One or two were even bold enough to ask him what progress he was making with the case. In the end, he escaped by letting himself out into the grounds. The last end of the last game was being played out in light that had already failed. One player was dangling his handkerchief so that the bowler could see the jack. Kenworthy moved right away from the fringe of the crowd, walked down into the shadow of the chestnuts and stood perfectly still, perfectly quiet.

It was actually a minutes or two after half past ten that he emerged from his retreat and made his way to the card room. Gibson was waiting to buttonhole him outside.

"I checked his keys. There wasn't one to *Notre Repos*."

"Good."

"And it interested him very much when he saw what line I was following. It made him very uncomfortable indeed."

"I'll bet it did. But you didn't get more out of him?"

"He volunteered nothing. And since you'd given me no adequate briefing—"

"All right, Inspector—don't shoot me down. I always hate this stage of a case."

"But you think that he might have had a key to the Bielbys' house?"

"He'd lived with the Bielbys for a few months after they first moved to Sandringham Avenue. I think that that's one of the reasons why Bielby made damned sure that he went to Borstal. But he'd certainly have a key—either because they gave him one, or because he got himself one cut. And he'd hang on to it. People of Cliff's mentality are always interested in other people's keys."

They went into the card room and there was an immediate cessation of all talk. But Kenworthy attempted no formal introduction of his purpose. He leaned forward and asked William Tunnicliffe how he was feeling. Tunnicliffe answered with an effort at nonchalance that was anything but convincing. His face was swollen and discoloured, his right eye closed, but he was stubbornly compelling himself to stay on the premises.

Then Kenworthy spoke casually to Mawdesley.

"It must have been a weird feeling, that night, being given a lift in a vintage car that used to be your own pride and joy."

The evening had had an effect on Mawdesley. He had drunk liberally. He had begun to accustom himself to the companionship of old cronies who were playing the social game of holding nothing against him. But Kenworthy's unexpected question made him uneasy.

"You just have to take things as they happen," he said.

"It's a pity you didn't tell us you'd been there that night. It would have saved us a lot of checking and cross-checking."

"I'm sorry."

Mawdesley managed a false chuckle.

"A man with my record doesn't go sticking his nose into things. I was nearly arrested in the marketplace not long ago, on suspicion of stealing a cauliflower."

False chuckling now from the assembled company. Kenworthy closed his eyes until it had died down.

"Cliff has filled us in on a lot of detail of what happened that night."

There was now universal silence, which Mawdesley seemed the least disposed to break.

"Why did you go back to *Notre Repos* after Cliff had driven you home?"

Kenworthy's tone was as gentle as that of one who expects the answer to be innocuous. For a split second it seemed that there was not going to be an answer at all. Then Mawdesley committed himself.

"I'd left my cigarette lighter on a coffee table. I'm always lost without it."

"A little late, wasn't it? After Maggie Bielby had told you she was going to bed?"

"I was sure she'd said that just to get rid of us."

"You're sure that it was to fetch your lighter that you went back? It wasn't in order to have another go at reasoning with her?"

Kenworthy turned and explained the situation amiably to the company.

"Cliff and Mawdesley, you see, had had a disconcerting chat with Maggie earlier in the evening. And you all know how upright Maggie was. She promised that she was going to set the police on the trail of certain activities. Because she had had as much of that sort of thing in her life as she was going to take. And that worried you, didn't it, Mawdesley? They couldn't get you for things that Bielby had been up to while you were inside. But one thing was going to lead to another, and something out of the past was going to be turned up for which you were likely to go inside again: a spot of unhealthy curiosity, perhaps, about one of your holding companies. Another spell on D landing was something you couldn't face, wasn't it?"

"I'm not staying here to be talked to like this."

Mawdesley stood up; but found policemen all round him.

"Sit down, Mawdesley. I will tell you how you came to go back to *Notre Repos*. And when I have finished, you need not say anything. But Sergeant Cooper will write down anything you do say, and it may be used in evidence. Because I am arresting you for the murder of Margaret Bielby. It was a moment of inspiration on your part, remembering that Cliff might still have a key—"

"I told you, I went back for my lighter."

"You walked back, and rang her doorbell, and Mrs. Bielby got out of bed and came down and answered it?" asked Kenworthy.

"She hadn't actually gone to bed. She was in her dressing-gown, making herself a milk drink."

"She must have been delighted to see you—having so recently asked you to leave."

"I simply told her I'd left the lighter, told her exactly where it was. She went and got it for me and I came away."

"Just like that?"

"I can't tell you anything but the truth."

"That," Kenworthy said, "is a statement that deserves to be worked in embroidery and framed on the wall. I'm afraid I prefer my version. You asked Cliff, quite casually, if he still had a key; and he had. He didn't ask you what you wanted with it; he preferred not to know. And you didn't tell him; this was one man's business and one man's work. You went indoors and got gloves. You walked back to Sandringham Avenue. You let yourself in with that key—and Maggie Bielby was in fact already in bed. When she heard you come in she thought you were her husband. You'd been a guest in their house very frequently in the old days, and you knew every little thing about his habits and temperament. You went through the lounge, upsetting a chair or two, pulling out a few books. Then you went into the kitchen, switched on the transistor radio, jammed the door with a couple of chairs."

Kenworthy got up and mimed a few movements in the centre of the room, exactly as he had acted out the scene in front of Gibson.

"You then went upstairs. There was no need for stealth, because Maggie still thought you were Bielby—until she saw you. Then you went for the gun, which was still where Bielby boasted he kept it. You then made her ring Lucy Fielding and ask to speak to Bielby. And she did that: looking up the nostril of an automatic pistol. She asked him to come home and deal with an urgent situation."

There was a stifled groan from William Tunnicliffe. He was breathing heavily with pain.

"So all you now had to do was wait for Bielby's footsteps to make themselves heard on the pavement outside. You fired before he entered the house, escaped while he was still looking for his wife in the kitchen."

Mawdesley did not speak. In his time he had been a formidable manager of men, but there was one prospect that paralysed his vocal chords.

"Take him away," Kenworthy said to Gibson. "And whatever keys you find on him or about his house, try them out at *Notre Repos*."

As Gibson led Mawdesley out a suppressed communal sigh stirred the card room of the Crown and Cushion Club.

"I fear we haven't finished yet," Kenworthy said.

"Because Mawdesley didn't kill Bielby. In some ways, maybe that's a pity."

William Tunnicliffe had been holding his face in his hands for the last few minutes. Now he started to struggle out of his chair.

"Chief Superintendent, you'll have to excuse me—"

"Could you bear with me just one more minute, please?"

Kenworthy made a barely perceptible signal, and Sergeant Cooper moved to William Tunnicliffe's side.

"You see, the man who shot Bielby was Maggie Leyland's father—mistakenly assuming that Bielby had shot her. But there were additional reasons for bad blood between Maggie Leyland's father and Bielby. They had to do with recent events on the Town Moor."

Kenworthy assumed a quizzical expression.

"It was a secret well kept—for a place that doesn't seem to be very clever with its secrets. There was a street party during the First World War, to launch a battalion on its way to France. Maggie Leyland's mother was helping with refreshments. Her father was there too: a man under contract to the estate landlord. It isn't for me to criticize the practical help he gave to those two women in his lifetime. Some people might think that sooner or later he ought to have acknowledged his daughter. But he knew best his own family dispositions: and the sensitive state of his own dignity. I don't think his brother William ever knew."

There was no need to wonder whether the murderer was going to admit himself. Herbert Tunnicliffe, the paternalist, unchallenged head of the family, dour, ruined and indefensible, was sitting with his hands trembling violently. His younger brother took his hands from his mutilated face and was seen to be weeping.

"I suppose you went out to the lavatory, or something, that morning, when the three of you were checking nails and screws. The nature of your errand wouldn't have entered your brother's or sister's minds. But they wouldn't want to add complications to life by admitting that you had ever left the room."

Kenworthy and Bartram walked together across the nocturnal town: nacreous street-lights freezing the façades of the Civic Trust High Street.

"Quite a Founders' Night," Bartram said. "I said it was going to be."

"*Notre Repos*, Superintendent."

NGAIO MARSH

BESTSELLING PAPERBACKS BY A "GRAND MASTER" OF THE MYSTERY WRITERS OF AMERICA.

____ARTISTS IN CRIME	0-515-07534-5/$3.50
____GRAVE MISTAKE	0-515-08847-1/$3.50
____HAND IN GLOVE	0-515-07502-7/$3.50
____DEATH IN A WHITE TIE	0-515-08591-X/$3.50
____DEATH IN ECSTASY	0-515-08592-8/$3.50
____DEATH OF A PEER	0-515-08691-6/$3.50
____PHOTO FINISH	0-515-07505-1/$3.50
____WHEN IN ROME	0-515-07504-3/$3.50
____A WREATH FOR RIVERA	0-515-07501-9/$3.50
____VINTAGE MURDER	0-515-08084-5/$3.50
____TIED UP IN TINSEL	0-515-07443-8/$3.50